	DATE	
160	14	
149	22	
103	23	
8	1	
150	33	
12	16	
132	35	
19	38	

The
South African
Quirt

Also by Walter D. Edmonds

※

ROME HAUL (1929)
THE BIG BARN (1930)
ERIE WATER (1933)
MOSTLY CANALLERS (1934)
DRUMS ALONG THE MOHAWK (1936)
CHAD HANNA (1940)
YOUNG AMES (1942)
IN THE HANDS OF THE SENECAS (1947)
THE WEDDING JOURNEY (1947)
THE FIRST HUNDRED YEARS (1948)
THEY FOUGHT WITH WHAT THEY HAD (1951)
THE BOYDS OF BLACK RIVER (1953)
THE MUSKET AND THE CROSS (1960)
THE ERIE CANAL (1960)

The
South African
Quirt

❧

Walter D. Edmonds

Little, Brown & Company
Boston ❧ *Toronto*

FIRST EDITION

Library of Congress Cataloging in Publication Data

Edmonds, Walter Dumaux, 1903–
    The South African quirt.

    I. Title.
PS3509.D564S6   1985   813'.52   84-27854
ISBN 0-316-21153-2

VB

Designed by Jeanne F. Abboud

Published simultaneously in Canada
by Little, Brown & Company (Canada) Limited

PRINTED IN THE UNITED STATES OF AMERICA

For my stepdaughter
Janet Baker-Carr Agoos
with love

The
South African
Quirt

ONE

✿ "You'd better be after getting the mail," Annie Doherty told him. "You know your father wants to have it the minute it comes."

She said this nearly every morning because Natty Dunston was, as she declared, better at putting things off than anybody she'd met in all her life, and as usual Natty nodded and said, "I know." He didn't see what business it was of Annie's when he went down to the river road to collect the letters from their rural box, but he didn't make an issue of it, because Annie was really the only person in the house he had to talk to.

Feeling unwell, his mother had returned to their home in New York City shortly after his birthday in July, taking his small sister with her. His older brother George was away on a series of visits to friends he had made in boarding school. So Natty and his father were, as Mr. Dunston liked to put it, holding the fort on the farm alone, with only Annie Doherty to look after them.

The farm stood on the east bank of the Black River, extending north and south for just a mile along the shore. There were over a thousand acres of fields and woods and pastures and flat sandy upland, and the nearest neighbor in either direction was a mile away. It was six miles to their post village of Boonville, located thirty miles north of Utica on the highway that led to Watertown and Lake Ontario beyond. To many people it seemed lonely country, lonelier in 1915 than it would today.

To Mr. Dunston it seemed heroic to live there with only Annie caring for them. He was inclined to associate himself with dramatic heroes of history and literature. Annie Doherty was a rather haphazard young woman when it came to using a duster or broom, but fortunately she was a splendid cook, which made it possible for Mr. Dunston to regard the dust with some tolerance while he and Natty held the fort in a thoroughly comfortable way.

But Mr. Dunston was not by nature a tolerant man. He had been fifty when he married — for the first time — and now, at sixty-four, there were periods in which he found the raising of three children and the worries and frustrations posed by his wife's fragile health difficult to bear. Though he was not a large man, he seemed to twelve-year-old Natty a very formidable person, especially when his opaque and piercingly blue eyes were questioning a dubious piece of childhood behavior.

That summer, instead of commuting between the city and the farm in upstate New York, Mr. Dunston had decided to bring his work up with him and at this time was writing a brief in an extremely complicated case in patent law, using the living room as his office. From breakfast until mid-afternoon he insisted on absolute quiet throughout the house. Natty came and went through Annie's kitchen and used the back stairs to get to his bedroom. He hardly ever saw his father except at meals.

"You'd better be after getting the mail," Annie reminded him.

"I'm going," Natty said, "but I've got to get Bingo first."

Bingo was at the bank of the brook (beyond which stood the farm buildings), watching bubbles as they floated down a long granite slide to the boiling pool at the back of the house. He was five

months old and of the slightly nondescript type
that people in the country referred to as shepherd.
Natty's mother had seen him on a neighboring
farm and had bought him for Natty's birthday.
Mr. Dunston disapproved. The dog, he said, was
only a mongrel. He did not want anything but
purebreds on his place, so get rid of him. But Mrs.
Dunston, to Natty's surprise, had stood her
ground.

"Natty needs to have a dog. This summer especially. When Bessie and I have left for New York
and with George away visiting most of the summer, he will need the companionship, if nothing
else."

"Well," Mr. Dunston said grudgingly. "He can
keep him for now. But he can't have him in the
house."

Of course, for a boy to have a dog he couldn't
bring indoors — to share his room, to sleep on the
foot of his bed where his feet could feel him in the
dark, most of all to go upstairs at bedtime down the
long hall to the back of the house — was to have
only half a dog. Bingo slept out in the cowbarn, in
a barrel propped on its side in one of the box stalls.
He was comfortable enough, and there was some
compensation for Natty in going outside every
morning to let him out, when Bingo greeted him
with almost a war dance of delight.

[*6*]

He did so now, when Natty came down the steps from the kitchen porch. They raced around to the front of the house, Bingo letting out three staccato barks as they passed the living-room windows. Natty cast back an apprehensive glance, but his father's face did not appear, and they pelted down the drive to the river road without hindrance.

The mailman had not yet come, so for a few minutes Natty looked for a grasshopper to throw in the brook where it ran under the road through an arched stone culvert. Trout hung in there. You didn't always see one take the hopper, but if the fish was any size his splash reverberated when he jumped. One did, above average size by the sound. Natty started to look for another grasshopper. Then up on the road Bingo barked.

Some days you could hear the hoofbeats on the planks of the bridge half a mile upriver, but Natty had been too absorbed listening for his trout to hear anything but the flow of water and the solid splash. He moved out of the shade of the alders and into the bright sunshine on the road.

The mailman's old white horse, hauling the buggy at a sleepy trot, was already in sight. Nobody could say for certain when it was that Mr. Lewis started using him on the mail route — a good many years longer ago than Natty was old — but

Natty had learned his name, anyhow. Mr. Lewis himself had told him it was Benjamin; and by now Benjamin knew every box on the route. He pulled to the side of the road and stopped exactly opposite the Dunstons' box, with the front wheel cramped a little to make things easier in case Mr. Lewis wanted to get out. When Benjamin heard the box lid close or when Mr. Lewis clucked his tongue, he would move ahead and gradually work up to his deliberate trot. He never started before he heard one of those two sounds. It was said Mr. Lewis never laid his hand on the reins once they got out of Boonville village.

Today Mr. Lewis was reading in the *Atlantic Monthly* magazine and he didn't look up until he had come to the end of a paragraph. Then he saw Natty beside the wheel, holding the letters to go, which he had taken out of the mailbox.

"Good morning, Natty," he said, accepting the letters and putting them into one pocket of the big mail pouch on the floor beside his feet. "Glad you were here to meet me or Benjamin and I would have to go up to the house. Got a package for Mr. Dunston that's got to be signed for, but you can do that."

He fished the letters for the house and the farm people out of the pouch, together with a newspaper and a catalogue. Then he reached under the seat for an odd-looking package, about four inches wide and thirty long.

"Queer shape for a package," Mr. Lewis observed. "And it's got interesting stamps." He peered at them through his glasses. "From South Africa."

He handed the package to Natty and both of them studied the stamps. "You don't see many like that in this part of the country. Fact is, I can't remember ever seeing a South African stamp before."

"I haven't, either," Natty said.

"Wouldn't mind having them to put in my stamp album," Mr. Lewis said.

"Do you collect stamps?" Natty asked.

"In a sort of way," Mr. Lewis replied.

"I'll see if I can get them for you," Natty offered, feeling a sudden friendliness towards Mr. Lewis.

He was an unusual man to find delivering mail on a rural route. He read only high-class magazines like the *Atlantic Monthly* or *Century* or *Scribner's*; and if they ran out of interest by the end of the month, he took along books from the classics. He was quite delicately made and always wore a suit and a necktie, even on hot summer days. "Quite gentlemanly for a Welshman," Mr. Dunston once said of him, the tone of his voice conveying the impression to Natty that he considered Welshmen as a whole to be distinctly otherwise.

"That would be good of you, Natty," Mr. Lewis said. "How's Bingo coming along?"

"He's fine, Mr. Lewis."

"He'll turn into quite a dog, I shouldn't wonder."

Mr. Lewis gave a click of his tongue and found his place in the *Atlantic Monthly* and Benjamin started on down the river road. Natty tucked the South African package into the crook of his arm, with the newspaper and the catalogue folded around it, and took the letters in his other hand.

It had grown very warm for an early September morning, so Natty took his time going up the drive. Before he got to the house, Mr. Dunston came out on the front verandah. Even at that distance Natty could see the blue of his father's eyes and imagined the disapproval behind them. It made him quicken his pace, his thin legs just short of running. His older brother George had once remarked, "Natty does not run. He scurries. Like a little spider."

"I take it the mail was late in coming," Mr. Dunston said, his voice on the rising note that invariably filled Natty with alarm.

"Mr. Lewis was a little late," Natty said. "And he talked for a few minutes after he got here."

"What about? I should have thought he would want to make up time," Mr. Dunston said.

"It was about this package for you, Daddy. It's from South Africa. Mr. Lewis was interested in the stamps. He keeps a stamp album."

"So I suppose he would like to keep the stamps. Is that it?"

"Yes," Natty answered.

"Well, he can. You can put them in an envelope and leave them in the box for him tomorrow."

A wave of relief swept over Natty. He had been going to tell his father the nice things Mr. Lewis had said about Bingo, but decided suddenly it would be much better not to. Mr. Dunston had taken the letters and the package, saying, "Come into the living room till I sort this mail and then you can take what's for the farm over. And tell Lincoln John I'll be out to talk to him after lunch."

Lincoln John was the farmer, and because there were also a teamster and a farmhand and a chore-boy to help on the place, Mr. Dunston liked to refer to him as "my superintendent." To Natty he was a big, silent man who listened to Mr. Dunston's orders about what was to be done and how he was to do it and then did it his own way and when it suited him. Though he liked Mr. John, Natty took the farm letters reluctantly, wanting to see his father open the package from South Africa. He ran at top speed, but by the time he got back Mr. Dunston had cut the string and unfolded the wrapping paper and was holding what seemed to be some kind of whip.

"It's a quirt," he told Natty. "It's from a lawyer in Johannesburg who presented my brief in the Eagle Brand case over there. Pieter Van Hoven. He says it's a quirt." Mr. Dunston picked up a piece of notepaper. "He says it's made from rhinoceros hide and will bring the most mean-minded horse to his senses with one stroke. It certainly feels like a powerful whip."

He held it out so Natty could see it. It was about thirty inches long, with a stiff leather hand-grip — not like the handles of buckhorn set at right angles on his father's English riding crops, which were hung in the deer horns over the small sofa. It was slimmer, and it had a flat lash, a foot or eighteen inches long, on the end. "It's no use to me with that lash," Mr. Dunston said.

"You could cut it off," Natty said. "I could cut it off for you."

Mr. Dunston agreed. "Cut it off so it's about three inches long. With the end cut square. Like the loop on the end of a crop. Do you understand?"

Natty said he did. It pleased him to have suggested a project his father approved of. There wasn't time to get it done before the lunch, but during the meal he pictured himself at work in the farm shop. He would have to be sure he had a sharp edge on the blade of his knife, and he became so preoccupied he only half listened to what his father was saying.

Mr. Dunston seemed to be in a state of some excitement. His normally high coloring was even redder than usual and his upturned mustache and white goatee looked almost electrically bristling.

"That quirt," he exclaimed. "It would have come in useful with Rocco."

"Who's Rocco?" asked Natty.

"He was a hammerheaded, long-legged roan horse. The men in Henderson's riding stable called him Rocco. They wouldn't let anyone take Rocco out unless they were sure he could handle him."

"Did you ever ride him?" Natty asked.

"Oh yes. I almost always had Rocco when I rode in Central Park. He started to act up the first time I mounted him, but I squeezed him between my thighs and made him squeal. I'm not a big man, " Mr. Dunston said modestly, "but I have enormous strength in my thighs and I've never been on a horse I couldn't make squeal if I chose to." Natty looked at him admiringly and with considerable awe as he continued. "Rocco was over sixteen hands and looked knobby and ungainly, but he could go like the wind. Mounted police would ride full tilt after us, thinking I was on a runaway. As a matter of fact, I made a practice of riding Rocco without stirrups — crossed them over the pommel — and if it comes to that, there might have been moments when Rocco thought he *was* out of my control. But he never really was. If I'd had that quirt then, the idea would never have crossed his mind."

Mr. Dunston broke off as Annie came in with their dessert, and for some reason not clear to himself, Natty felt hugely relieved. His father's voice had dropped back to normal as he told Annie that the apple pie was strictly up to her standard. They finished the meal and made their way across the brook to the farm, Mr. Dunston to look for Mr. John at the farmhouse and Natty heading for the shop with the quirt in his hand.

The farm shop was all across one end of a large building that housed the farm machinery. As Natty worked at the twelve-foot bench set under a west window so that the early afternoon sunlight came in on his head and shoulders, he was conscious of the mowing machines, plows, and harrows at his back. There were also the huge shapes of the George Wood reaper and binder that harvested the oats and buckwheat, and of the McCormick corn-harvester that cut and bound the silage corn, bringing the ten- to fifteen-foot stalks back into its jaws like some predatory dinosaur and casting out the bound bundles behind it. A three-horse team was required to pull either of these machines; even the great dapple gray, half-Percheron team found them too heavy. The machines stood waiting, portentous and ominous, and always when he was alone in the shop Natty had a sense of them possessing life of their own — as if suddenly they could take upon themselves the running of the farm, ruling not only the animals but the people as well. He had once mentioned this to his mother, but when Mr. Dunston heard about it he exploded. Natty dreamed too much; he ought to do useful work about the place instead of wandering off with that mongrel puppy, Lord knew where. Machines were only machines, objects that had to be stored and sheltered from the weather, which was why Mr. Dunston had given the building the somewhat grandiloquent name of Machinery Hall.

Natty put the quirt down on the bench and found the honing stone on a shelf at the back. It was a dark red waterstone, not like the oilstone Mr. Dunston had in the closet off the living room that he call the toolroom. Mr. John said a waterstone was every bit as good and saved using oil. Natty laid it down on the bench after he had dipped it in the pail that stood on the floor underneath. He opened the blade of his knife and began sharpening it with the circular motion Mr. John had shown him how to use: six times towards you and then turn the blade over and six times away, taking all the pains he could to hold the edge at a proper angle. Sunlight came through the window above the bench. A bluebottle bucketed round and round it, bouncing indiscriminately against the panes and sash, and the sound of the fly along with the rhythmic circular motions of his hand holding the knife so nearly put Natty to sleep that he did not hear Mr. John come into the building — not until he said, "What are you up to, Natty?"

Natty explained about cutting the lash of the quirt to make it look more like a crop. Mr. John picked it up, flexing it gently. He was a big man, a great deal taller than Mr. Dunston and proportionately broader across the shoulder. He spoke softly and moved slowly; Natty admired and looked up to him.

"It's a powerful whip," Mr. John remarked. "I don't know any horse mean enough to want to hit him with it. Where'd your father get it?"

"It came from a man in South Africa," Natty told him.

"I don't know much about South Africa," Mr. John said in his deliberate way, putting the crop back down on the bench. "Don't know nothing about those people, and if it comes to that, I'm not sure I would want to. That's a wicked piece of leather to my way of thinking. Your pa is right, though, about taking off the lash. The real power lies in the stem." He took Natty's knife and tested the blade with his thumb. "You've put a nice edge on it," he said. "Real nice."

Natty felt the skin on his back wrinkle with pleasure. In his rather feckless existence it wasn't often that a bit of praise came his way. "I want to make a neat job," he said.

"Well," Mr. John said. "If you was to ask me I think I'd use a square and draw my blade along it, like a straightedge."

He took the square off the nail it was hanging on and demonstrated, unobtrusively bearing down on it to keep it from budging while Natty drew his knife blade along its edge. It was very satisfying to see how easily and cleanly the blade sliced through the lash.

"You think it's all right?" he asked, holding it up for Mr. John to inspect.

"I do," Mr. John said. "I couldn't have done it any better myself."

His approval made Natty feel so fine that he got up his nerve to ask a question he had never dared to ask before but had been bothering him ever since Mr. John came to take charge of the farm.

"Why have you got your last name first, Mr. John?"

Mr. John seemed neither surprised nor disturbed by Natty's question.

"My father's name was Robert John," he replied. "So my last name is John."

"Well," Natty said, "Lincoln is a last name — like Abraham Lincoln. If it was me I would change my name to John Lincoln, I think."

Mr. John looked down at him for a moment.

"Boys can't change their names just like that. Girls can do it by getting married and then have their husband's name, though sometimes the name they get isn't as good a one as their own, and sometimes the man they get isn't as good as his name. I guess it would be possible for me to go to a judge and get my names switched, but I don't want to. My pa named me Lincoln for the man you just named, Natty, and that's good enough for me."

Natty could see that Mr. John did not want to go on with the discussion, so he thanked him for helping with the quirt and said he hoped he hadn't said anything to upset Mr. John.

"Not at all," Mr. John said equably, and they left the shop together. Mr. John went to see to some job on the farm while Natty headed over the brook to the big house. He knocked on the living-room door and went in. His father was working at his desk and Natty gave him the quirt.

Mr. Dunston examined it and said it would do very well. He laid it on the side of the desk, then changed his mind and took it over to the deer horns and hung it with his riding crops.

"I've got to finish this brief by tomorrow," he said. "So don't disturb me till suppertime."

Natty took the hint and left. Time hung on his hands and after a while he joined Bingo outdoors. They wandered down to one of the oat fields, where the shocks, like Indian tepees, stood irregularly over the stubble. Bingo often found mice inside them. He would work his way in between the bundles and there would be a commotion. Sometimes Natty would go in after the puppy. Mr. Dunston disapproved of his doing so because, he said, it loosened the shocks, but Mr. John did not object.

Inside the shock it was dusty from Bingo's scurry to catch mice. The puppy, as a matter of fact, was licking his muzzle elaborately, as if he had caught one or more. If he had, he would throw them up later. But now he sat down against Natty's leg and they looked out together through the narrow opening they had made in entering. At the far end of the field, the second farm team had appeared hauling the hay wagon, and Benson, the teamster, and Roy, the farmhand, were beginning to load the sheaves. When they reached Natty's shock, they would take the sheaves away from each side, leaving him and Bingo sitting in the open field. They might offer a comment or they might not. It made no difference at the moment, because they would have a full load before they reached him.

He watched the two men and the team with detached indifference. Benson finished topping the load and turned the team towards the barn. The field was empty. Bingo suddenly made retching noises and Natty told him to get out. "Out! Out-*side!*" he commanded, his voice rising as the margin of safety noticeably decreased. But Bingo obliged in time, walking on stiff legs through the opening between the sheaves, his muzzle pointed rigidly forward and abruptly ejecting the bodies of two small mice, which, as they fell between the stubble, were instantly covered with sandy dust. Putting his nose down to them, the puppy evidently contemplated re-eating them but fortunately decided otherwise and returned to Natty inside the shock, wagging his tail, plainly consumed with a sense of his nonexemplary behavior.

They sat on, companionably content in their mutual absence of thought, until the team backed the hay wagon out of the loft floor, were unhitched, and took their own way to the stable. After a while the clang of the farmhouse supper bell, vigorously swung by Mrs. John, came across the field, and almost immediately after, the harsh tin blast that meant it was time for Natty to come back to get ready for dinner. Mr. Dunston was insistent on punctuality, especially on the part of minor members of the family, and also demanded that his children take a bath and change into clean clothes before joining him at the dining table. A handbell like Mrs. John's was available to Annie Doherty, but she preferred the doryman's foghorn that Mrs. Dunston had once brought back from a visit to relatives in Maine. Its abrupt shattering of the afternoon stillness infuriated Mr. Dunston, but Annie was not to be deterred from using it.

"How else would the boy know it was time to come in?" she would demand in fearless confrontation of her employer. "A bell here. A bell there. It would muddle the head of the Holy Father Himself!"

She met Natty at the kitchen door with a bowl full of table scraps for Bingo's supper. Natty accepted it and took it back down the steps to the lawn. Bingo, an overenthusiastic gobbler of food, was apt to cast a lot of it over the rim of his bowl, and Annie objected to cleaning up the porch after him. Leaving the puppy at his supper, Natty went up to change.

Dinner always put his natural behavior under considerable strain, and the more so when he and his father were alone together. Most of the meal passed in silence. No burst of chatter occurred as it sometimes did when Mrs. Dunston occupied the other end of the table. Then, because Natty was an excitable small boy, any anecdote he launched forth on was apt to emerge from his mouth not in talk, as Mr. Dunston pointed out, but as pure gabble, and consequently was quenched as quickly as possible. If Natty persisted, he was often sent away from the table to ponder the virtues of silence upstairs in his bedroom. Only Annie Doherty, bringing in the next course, had anything to say this evening, however, and neither Natty nor his father paid much attention to her. As soon as they had finished dessert they went into the living room.

There, the silence between them seemed easier. Mr. Dunston sat down at his desk to write a letter, and Natty, as he did most evenings, picked up one of the four-volume set of *Pictures from Punch*, which he found endlessly entertaining, especially a series depicting the sporting misadventures of three bungling fellows named Brown, Jones, and Robinson. He carried the book over to the center table and pulled up a chair — resentfully, because his older brother was allowed to look at the books while holding them in his lap. Mr. Dunston considered Natty too small to handle them properly — they were slightly bigger than quarto ("elephant quarto," Mr. Dunston liked to call them) — and he had issued an edict that Natty must open them on a table if he was to look at them at all. Otherwise he might crack the book's spine. ("Spine" was a word that came frequently into Mr. Dunston's conversation, and he was apt to say that spine was an attribute Natty conspicuously lacked.)

The volume Natty had chosen fell open at an episode about the three inept companions on a stag hunt in Scotland, and almost at once he began to giggle. Becoming suddenly aware that he was doing so, he looked up to see whether he had annoyed his father, who considered giggling to be a silly, girlish trait and therefore abominable in a boy.

Though Mr. Dunston had in fact turned from his letter writing, he was not looking in the direction of his son. Instead he was staring at the deer horns on the opposite wall, where the South African quirt rested among the English riding crops. His face was strangely absorbed. The phrase "lost in thought" popped into Natty's head. It seemed to him as if his father's mind had wandered into some dark labyrinth at whose heart a brooding Minotaur stood waiting, and without knowing why, he felt a shiver fingering his spine.

He lowered his glance so that his father should not become aware that he was being watched, but the pictures of the three bumbling stag hunters meant nothing now. He felt alone, sealed from the world, in a stillness so profound that he only dimly heard his father clear his throat — which in itself was odd, for Mr. Dunston cleared his throat with the reverberating authority with which a military commander might call for a charge of cavalry. Natty had a sensation of desperately scrambling back into life and was surprised suddenly to find himself seated at the living-room table with the open volume of *Pictures from Punch* in front of him.

"I said, I am writing your mother, and I repeat, have you any message you'd like to send her?"

Mr. Dunston's blue stare was now riveted on Natty, who squirmed as he tried to find his voice. When it came it was high-pitched and hoarse and sounded strange even to himself.

"Yes. Send her my love. And say I miss her very much. And Bessie too."

His father's eyes still held him in their stare.

"Is that all you want me to tell her?" he asked. "Don't you want her to know what you've been doing with yourself?"

"No," Natty started to reply, but then thought it would be safer to say something. "Tell her . . . Tell her I had a good time with Bingo. He caught two mice in one of the oat shocks and then came out and sicked them up."

"I won't tell Mother that. It's not anything she'd

like to hear about," his father said. "Can't you think of something nicer?"

"No," Natty said. "Just tell her *I* miss her."

"What do you mean by that? Saying *I* as if you were the only one who missed her. Don't you think I miss her too?" Mr. Dunston's voice rose with each question. "How do you think a man feels when his wife so often has to leave him because of her poor health? I don't know why she has to go away. She's relatively young, compared to me. *I* don't have to go running back all the time to *my* New York doctor. I don't leave my wife. She leaves me!"

His voice kept rising as he spoke. Natty had never heard it quite like that before; it made him think of a person or maybe an animal tied and straining to get free. Not knowing what to say, he kept still, his eyes on the open pages of the book without seeing it at all. However, when his father spoke again, his voice seemed more nearly natural.

"I'm going to write a note to Mrs. Hollins," he said. "I want you to take it down tomorrow right after breakfast and wait for her answer."

The Hollinses were the Dunstons' nearest neighbors, a mile down the river road. Mr. Hollins worked a small, not very productive farm and Mrs. Hollins, to eke out their precarious income, came once a week to do the Dunston family wash. She was a small, perky, always busy woman who invariably made Natty think of a wren. He wondered what his father would have to write her for. Mr. Dunston explained.

"Your mother wrote me in her letter that came yesterday that Annie's mother has been to see her. Annie's old father is very ill and her mother wants her to come back to New York. She asked your mother to write — she cannot write herself. I must find out if Mrs. Hollins will cook for us if Annie leaves."

"She'll probably have to leave, won't she?" Natty asked.

"Yes, probably."

"What does she say?" Natty felt panic, like advancing fog, close in on him. Annie was the only person in the house he could talk to without constraint. He couldn't conceive of living there without her cheerful presence.

"I haven't told her about Mother's letter yet," Mr. Dunston replied. "That will have to wait till I've heard from Mrs. Hollins."

"But it's not fair not to tell her!" Natty cried, now taking sides, as it were, against his own wishes.

He saw his father stiffen.

"Are you suggesting that I'm acting unfairly?"

"No. I don't know. I mean if her father's so sick, oughtn't she to know it right away?"

"It's very likely he isn't all that ill," Mr. Dunston said. "Irish people are given to exaggerating things. They always give the worst side of any situation. They enjoy the excitement of it, in my opinion. No, Natty, I'll be the judge of when to tell Annie about her father."

He turned to the desk and began his note to Mrs. Hollins. After a minute Natty closed his volume of *Pictures from Punch;* it no longer appealed to him. "I think I'll go to bed," he told his father.

"Very well," Mr. Dunston said. "Bring your candle and I'll light it for you."

It was Mr. Dunston's expressed conviction that Natty was too feckless to be trusted with matches. Kerosene lamps were used to light the downstairs rooms, but none were allowed upstairs except for Mr. and Mrs. Dunston's own bedroom. The hazards of an overturned lamp in the middle of the night with kerosene igniting was a spectacle to which Mr. Dunston could bring enormous dramatic excitement whenever he conjured it up, as he not infrequently did. So Natty, in contrast to his brother George, had to have his own candle lighted for him, with the matches being retained. In that way, when he blew out his candle all possibility of fire would be eliminated and Mr. Dunston could sleep easy.

He now touched the flame to Natty's candlewick and shook out the match with a flourish.

"There you are, Natty. Good night."

Natty said good night in return, went out into the hall, and started up the stairs. In the dark, with just his candle, it seemed a much longer way to his room than it did in daylight and the house about him was suddenly enlarged. Strictures that had come his way in the course of the day, or in previous days, went with him, and during his passage down the long and narrow hall from the stair head to his bedroom at the back of the house, he became guiltily aware of his shortcomings. He felt himself surrounded by dangers deriving not only from his perpetrations but from nameless, more shadowy threats that grow in darkness everywhere for small and lonely beings.

His bedroom, when at last he reached it and closed and bolted the door, represented safety, though safety depended on certain precautions. Every evening before supper he fetched a chamber pot, which he had found disused in the attic, from the rear corner of his clothes closet, where it was hidden behind his rubber boots, and put it under his bed, because to leave his room in the middle of the night was to invite further incalculable risks. Then, from beneath his winter underwear in the bottom drawer of his bureau, he got a box of safety matches (when the fall days turned cold, he kept the matches under his summer underclothes) and stowed the box under his pillow. With these precautions, when at last he blew his candle out, he had transformed his room into a fort — a fort still under siege, to be sure, by the menaces of darkness, but one in which he could hope to survive until the graying dawn began to show in his east window.

He got up almost at once, then, to return the matchbox to the bureau drawer and to empty and wash out the chamber pot before hiding it again behind his rubber boots. Back in bed once more, his body felt soothed. He lay luxuriating in daylight safety and soon dozed off with all fears erased from his mind.

TWO

❧ NATTY was waked the second time by the aroma of roasting coffee beans and presently the harsh grating noise of the coffee grinder as Annie worked the crank. It was a cheerful sound and reassuring to a small boy just getting out of bed. He dressed himself in the sunlight flooding through the window, went to the bathroom to pass a dampened toothbrush across his teeth, and headed for the front stairs at the end of the long hall. The door to his parents' room was closed but he could hear his father singing the toreador's song from *Carmen* at the top of his voice in the bathroom beyond. Natty had learned from experience that this was a good augury of Mr. Dunston's mood, at least for the earlier part of the day.

Annie had heard the singing from the foot of the stairs. "It sounds as if the Mister is fine today," she observed to Natty. This was fortunate. Mr. Dunston demanded a cold baked apple for his breakfast every day of the year, but of course during the summer none were to be had and he was invariably disgruntled. But if he came down in a singing mood, there was hope for his getting through the morning meal in a tolerable emotional state. Natty agreed with Annie's appraisal.

"I think things went right for him in the bathroom," he said, which turned out to be the case. Mr. Dunston arrived at the breakfast table still in his buoyant mood and accepted a dish of dried apricots and apples from Annie without complaint. Past that hurdle the rest of the meal always went smoothly because it was always the same: oatmeal and thick cream from the farm (though Mr. Dunston disapproved of his son's using sugar instead of salt, as he himself preferred) and a poached egg on toast, bacon, and two corner pieces from the pan of fresh cornbread. Mr. Dunston liked everything to be familiar.

"Praised be to God," Annie whispered as Natty

started past to follow his father to the living room. Mr. Dunston gave him the letter to Mrs. Hollins.

"Don't fool around on your way," he said. "But don't be impatient if she takes a while before she gives you her answer. People like the Hollinses sometimes find it difficult to put a message down on paper. She shouldn't be badgered."

Natty had no intention of doing that. He liked being at the Hollinses' place; he felt more at ease there than he did at home. Their son Herschel, who was two years older than himself, he regarded as the best friend he had. Some Sundays, when he went there to visit, Herschel would be allowed time off from work and they would have the afternoon free, to wander in the woods, taking their lunch with them. Herschel knew a lot more about woods and about how to look for things than Natty, though Herschel always said his father knew more than he did or was ever likely to learn. His father could even talk to animals, wild as well as tame, so they understood him. Norman Hollins was a slight, lean, silent man, with his hair and mustache almost the same brown as his leathery skin; he didn't look exceptional in any way, but if Herschel said he could do such things, Natty believed him.

"Remember," Mr. Dunston now reiterated, "when Mrs. Hollins does give you a reply, you come straight home. Don't go wandering into the woods or playing around. I want her answer just as soon as I can get it."

"I know," Natty said and put the letter into his pocket, but he thought to himself that it was Annie who ought to know at once.

He went to the barn to get Bingo. A moment later, as they pelted around the corner of the house, he saw his father looking out at them through the living-room window. Around the corner, though, was out of sight, and out of sight was out of mind, and as they turned onto the river road, he dropped into a walk while Bingo, keeping well ahead, scouted from one side to the other.

Where the road curved away from the river, Natty left it and climbed the wooded bank to come up on the Hollinses' house from the back. He preferred this route, not only because it was shorter than going around by the road, but because he could use Herschel's secret path. Herschel claimed nobody but himself knew about it until he showed it to Natty, not even his sister Lois. It began fifteen or twenty feet inside the fringe of trees and ended well short of the Hollinses' home meadow. The thing about keeping it secret, Herschel told Natty, was never to go into the woods at exactly the same place, but the path itself, once you were on it, was well trimmed and without a stick on the ground from one end to the other. An Indian wouldn't even know it was there or hear someone passing along it. Even Bingo, who in his eagerness to be ahead had gone on along the road, was bewildered by Natty's sudden disappearance and had to sniff out his tracks; but then, once he had caught up, he resumed his place in the lead with a fine display of nonchalance.

Mrs. Hollins was making doughnuts when Natty came up the back steps and pushed through the kitchen door. He said, "Good morning, Mrs. Hollins," remembering to take his cap off, and pulled the letter from his pocket. "My father said to give you this and please to let me take an answer back."

Mrs. Hollins picked a doughnut out of the kettle of simmering fat and laid it on a rack beside a dozen others. "Your pa writing me a letter?" she asked in a voice of surprise. "Why did he do that, Natty?"

She wiped her hands on her apron and found her spectacles on the shelf above the sink. It wasn't like the sink in the Dunstons' kitchen; instead of white enamel with hot and cold water running out of faucets, it was worn, dark soapstone with a pump at one end. The Hollinses had to dip what hot water they needed from the tank at one end of the stove. But Mrs. Hollins's doughnuts tasted better than any Natty had ever eaten. When she had her spectacles on her nose, he asked if he might have one and she said, "Help yourself, Natty."

It was still warm, it tasted nutty and sweet, and the outside was flaked with particles that had a shine. Mrs. Hollins had once told him it was because she only made doughnuts when her husband had butchered a pig and brought her the new leaf lard. There was nothing like it for frying doughnuts or baking a chocolate cake. Now she looked up from reading Mr. Dunston's letter and told Natty, "You can have another if you like, and take one to Herschel in the barn, but tell Mr. Hollins if he'll come to the house. I want to ask him something."

Mr. Hollins was not in the barn but in his workshop, which had an anvil and forge in one corner and a long workbench against the wall. He was busy riving shingles from a block of white pine. For a minute Natty forgot his message from Mrs. Hollins and stood riveted by the spectacle of the neat, quick blows of Mr. Hollins's mallet against the back of the froe and the half-inch slabs falling free of the block. Afterwards the slabs would be shaved into shingles. Herschel had once told him that his father as a young man was said to be a top-notch hand at shingle shaving, finishing more than two bundles in a day, which amounted to over four hundred shingles. It seemed strange to Natty that such a quiet-seeming man could ever have maintained such a pace for a day. He was bemused, and when the quick blows of the mallet on the froe suddenly broke off, he was startled to hear Mr. Hollins ask, "Did you want to tell me something?"

Natty flushed guiltily as he gave Mr. Hollins his wife's message, but Mr. Hollins only smiled and allowed he might as well go up to the house. Perhaps she would give him a doughnut too, he said. Natty headed for the barn.

It was an old building with weathered vertical siding and built into the sidehill. The only light came through windows on each side of the door and two smaller ones in the wall over the cattle stanchions. It was dark compared to the big dairy barn on the Dunstons' place, which had windows along each wall the full length of the building. But Herschel maintained that the Hollinses' barn was good for their little herd of ten cows — easy to keep warm in winter, cool to milk in in summer. And to Natty it did indeed seem a snug place in spite of being so dark.

Herschel had just finished the daily cleaning-out and was glad to have the doughnut Natty brought him. "Ain't you going to eat yours?" he asked.

"I've already had one," Natty said, breaking his second in two. "We'll divide this one."

"I'll give my half to Redskin," Herschel said,

starting towards the back of the barn. Natty followed. On one side were two horse stalls and on the other a box stall that Herschel said was for borning. Beyond, the light was so dim that it took a minute or two for Natty's eyes to adjust sufficiently to make out Redskin lying in a bed of hay.

The dog was glad to have visitors. Natty could hear his tail patting the hay. Herschel offered him a piece of doughnut and he took it — though, it seemed to Natty, more out of politeness than with enthusiasm. When Bingo came charging in to find them and discovered the old dog and started making a complete check, nosing him all over, Redskin did not object but just lay quietly in his nest of hay, allowing the puppy to sniff his fill.

Looking down at them, Natty could not help thinking of the way he had last seen Redskin going after a heifer who was trying to stray. The dog was like a red streak among the brake-ferns. In no time, his jaws snapping, he had overtaken the heifer. Herschel said that Redskin never bit the cows, but they got the message. He never let one get away once he had started them home for the barn.

"Always knowed when it was time to fetch them," Herschel said, and Natty had seen the little dog often enough starting alone up the sandy hill to the flat where the daytime pasture was. If Redskin could not find one cow, he brought the rest back to the gate, and when they had been let through to the barn, he would start off back up the hill and hunt until he found the stray.

"Is he sick?" Natty asked.

"Pa says it's his old age has caught up with him," Herschel replied.

"How old is he?"

"I don't exactly know. He was getting the cows when I started going out to the barn to help with feeding," Herschel said. "Fifteen, maybe sixteen. I don't know. All I know is I have got to get the cows from now on."

He grinned a little, but Natty could tell he wasn't too glad to add that job to all the other chores he was expected to do.

"You ought to get another dog and teach him to work like Redskin," he said.

"Not easy to find a dog that smart," Herschel said.

The old dog had had enough of Bingo's sniffs. He raised his head from the hay and his upper lip curled back to show his teeth. He mildly growled. As a heifer would, Bingo got the message and backed off. The boys heard Mr. Hollins calling from the house porch.

"Wants you to come," Herschel said. "I got to stay here and finish up."

With Bingo trotting ahead, Natty returned to

the Hollinses' house. Mrs. Hollins said she had a
letter for him to give his father.

"You better start right off," she told him. "Your
pa says he wants an answer soon as possible."

Natty put it in his pocket and went out down
the meadow to find Herschel's secret path, came
out on the river road, and headed home; but half
along the way he remembered he hadn't been to
see the white-pine stumps in quite a while, and he
turned off the road to find them. There were half a
dozen of them left, spaced far apart among the
newer stand of spruce and balsam. Virgin pines,
according to Mr. Dunston. Herschel said they
must have been cut in a winter of deep snow, for
the sawed tops of the stumps were almost six feet
above the ground. Natty had never anywhere seen
stumps so large. One of them, which he headed for
now, was eight feet across. Herschel had cut steps
in the side of it with his axe so you could climb up
onto it, which Natty did when he reached it.
Standing on top made him feel important. Like an
Indian chief. He began stamping his heels and,
treading a tight circle, let out cries he imagined to
be like war whoops, while the puppy pranced
around the base, barking his head off. It was a
splendid moment. Natty had a sense of belonging
to those woods, of having a place in the world, of
fitting into the scheme of life. He never felt that
way at home.

Through his shouts he was vaguely aware of the sound of a wagon passing along the road, but he paid no attention to it, and for five minutes more continued his war dance. Then suddenly remembering Mrs. Hollins's letter, he decided he had better get home.

He had hardly come out on the river road when he saw the mailman's old white horse plodding towards him. Mr. Lewis was reading as usual and had to drop his book to seize the reins and pull Benjamin to a halt — the horse did not consider stopping between mailboxes the proper thing to do.

"How are you, Natty?"

"Fine, thank you," Natty said.

Mr. Lewis looked at him with a questioning expression that Natty found disquieting. It was not unkind; it was more as if something was worrying Mr. Lewis.

"Your pa was at the mailbox when I and Benjamin came along," Mr. Lewis said. "I was surprised. He doesn't usually come down to pick up his mail."

"No," Natty said. "I'm supposed to get it."

"Then," Mr. Lewis said in his gentle voice, "maybe you'd better get home as quick as you can."

He clicked his tongue at Benjamin — needlessly, because the old horse had started up of his own accord. Natty set off at a dead run — with

Bingo racing beside him, uttering cheerful yelps. It was obvious now that they had spent a good deal more time in the woods than Natty had intended, which meant that his father would be displeased and maybe angry as well.

His apprehension was confirmed when he started up the driveway. Mr. Dunston was standing on the front porch and Natty could see the piercing blue of his eyes under the brim of his white felt hat. Natty's feet began to drag, and when he reached the foot of the porch steps, it was only with an effort of will that he managed to raise his eyes.

"You are late," Mr. Dunston said. His white mustache, which he wore turned up at the tips like the Kaiser's, was vibrant with disapproval.

"Yes." Natty had difficulty finding his voice. "I'm sorry. I had to wait for Mrs. Hollins to write the letter."

"When did she give it to you?"

"I don't know," Natty said. "I was at Hollinses' quite a while. I went to the barn to see Herschel. Old Redskin was sick."

"Never mind about Redskin," his father said. "When she did give you the letter, you came straight home? As I told you?"

"I started right away," Natty said. He tried to say it offhand, but under Mr. Dunston's bleak stare he had to drop his eyes.

[*41*]

"You didn't go wandering off in the woods?" Mr. Dunston persisted.

"No." He could hear his voice falter but his father broke in before he had a chance to say more.

"How is it then that Jody coming home with the milk wagon heard someone shouting and yelling in the woods? He said it sounded like you yelling like an Indian."

"I don't know," Natty said. "I went in with Bingo, but only for a little."

"What were you doing?"

"I got up on one of those big pine stumps to dance."

"So it was you Jody heard?"

"I guess so," Natty admitted.

"Then you lied to me," Mr. Dunston said, his voice very precise and cold. "Didn't you?"

"I — I didn't mean to."

Even as the words came from his mouth, he knew they were not a good answer. He was miserably aware of his father's stiff, upright figure and the contempt in the blue eyes.

"There is nothing worse than a chronic liar," Mr. Dunston was saying. "I will not allow it. You are continually telling lies, about what you do or don't do, about the fish you claim to have almost caught. It's unmanly. It's cowardly. If you lie to me again, just once more, I am going to punish you. I mean really punish you." He drew a harsh breath. "Did you bring Mrs. Hollins's letter?"

"Yes. I did."

"Then let me have it," Mr. Dunston said.

As he felt in his pockets, Natty had a moment of panic, thinking he might have lost it, but then he found it and handed it up to his father, finding the blue eyes still fixed on him. But to his enormous relief he saw his father relax as he read the letter.

"Mrs. Hollins can come and do for us," he said. "Good. I shall talk to Annie right away. Go ask her to come to the living room."

Natty hurried to the kitchen with his message. Annie put the pan of country sausage pats on the end of the stove, wiped her hands on her apron, and took it off. "What in the name of God will he be wanting to see me for now?" she demanded, sounding flustered.

"He's waiting. I think it's important," Natty told her and followed her into the living room.

His father was standing with his back to the fireplace, beneath the large engraving of Landseer's *Monarch of the Glen*. Mr. Dunston frequently assumed this position when he had something serious to say to an employee. The portentous figure of the huge stag above his head fortified the importance of what it was that he might have to say now; in front of him, Annie's stout body seemed, in Natty's eyes, suddenly to shrink.

"I'm afraid," Mr. Dunston said, clearing his throat, "I have sad news for you."

"Oh my God!" It was a whisper and perhaps only Natty heard her.

"I've had a letter from Mrs. Dunston, Annie. She writes that your mother came to see her and said your father was very unwell, and asking to see you."

"Oh my God," Annie said again, this time aloud, and in her distress reverting to her earlier brogue. "Is it dying he is, Misther Dunston?"

"My wife does not say, but she writes" — and Mr. Dunston held up the letter he had in his hand — "that she thinks you ought to come home right away."

"Oh, the poor old man!" Annie cried. "Yes I must." And then she re-collected herself. "But what will you and Natty be doing to look after yourselves?"

"Don't worry, Annie. Maybe Mrs. Hollins can come to cook for us. Very likely Mrs. John will help out. The main thing is for you to pack your things so Jody can drive you over to catch the afternoon train. You'll have to change in Utica for the train to New York, but you've done that before. I shall give you money for your tickets along with your wages. Also I'll give you money to take a cab from Grand Central because you'll be getting in pretty late."

To Natty's astonishment, Annie dropped a curtsy, thanking Mr. Dunston three or four times over, with "Oh, it's the kind man you are!" and "Blessed be to you!" and other grateful phrases until, coming to herself, she said she would put luncheon on the table and go straight off to pack.

Natty found himself bemused by her exclamations and excited apprehension, but still more by the way his father had broken the news to her — and especially how he had spoken about Mrs. Hollins: as if he had not yet read her note saying she would come to cook for them. Natty puzzled about this all through luncheon, during which Annie came in twice to thank his father all over again. It was not until he had gone upstairs to his room that a glimmer of understanding of Mr. Dunston's reason for speaking as he had occurred to him. Plainly, his father had not wanted Annie to realize that he had let a full day go by before he had told her about it. Mr. Dunston had in fact contrived to give the impression that the letter had arrived only in this morning's mail. In a small boy, Natty could see, this might well have been considered lying. He was still puzzling about it when the thud of hoofs on the bridge over the brook warned him that Jody had come with the spring wagon to take Annie to the station.

The kitchen, when he reached it, was boiling with commotion. Annie and Mrs. John stood by the stove in close conversation. Annie's voice pitched high with her anxieties and doubts while Mrs. John tried to reassure her. In the midst of their talk Mr. John came out of the back hall carrying Annie's portmanteau of black leather with brown straps buckled tight. It was so bulging big that Natty did not see how Annie could possibly get it off the train at Utica, let alone carry it to another platform for the New York express. Mr. John himself, for all his size, had some trouble getting it through the door to the porch and down the steps.

At that moment Mr. Dunston appeared with an envelope containing Annie's wages and money for her trip.

"I'm sure you'll find there's enough, Annie," he said. "If there isn't, Mrs. Dunston will make it up."

"Oh, thank you, sir," she said, stuffing it all so haphazardly into her handbag that to Natty it did not seem possible she could keep from losing it.

"I think Jody is ready for you," Mr. Dunston said, looking out of the window.

"Yes, to be sure," Annie exclaimed, adjusting her hat, which she wore perfectly straight. As she settled herself on the wagon seat, she looked to Natty the picture of intense respectability, yet at the same time rather lost and frightened. But, remembering herself, she called out, "Good-bye, Misther Dunston," and just as Jody took in on the reins, "Good-bye, Natty."

The horse started so suddenly that she was nearly jerked off the seat, which had no back; but she recovered herself at once and was again upright before the wagon turned the corner of the lawn. That was how Natty remembered her in the weeks to come: erect beside Jody, her hat sitting straight on her head, until the wagon vanished among the trees by the river. With her leaving, a new stillness seemed to invade the house, and little by little he became obsessed by its nighttime emptiness as only he and his father moved along the dark halls to occupy their rooms.

THREE

❦ THE FIRST SUPPER after Annie's departure was a silent one. Mr. Dunston and Natty usually found little to say to each other; it had been Annie, bustling in and out to change plates, who brought some sense of liveliness with her comments and chatter. Still, it didn't seem yet that she was quite gone. She had managed to find time to leave a cold supper — Mrs. John had helped Natty set it out, carving lamb off a cold leg and slicing tomatoes that Annie had dipped in boiling water to peel them the way Mr. Dunston liked — and a lemon jelly for dessert with thick cream from the farm.

Mr. Dunston said approvingly that it had been a good supper but he added, "We can't expect meals like Annie's from now on. Mrs. Hollins is a decent woman and she's done quite nicely for your mother and me when we've been up here for spring fishing. But, of course, she had Mother here to tell her how to do things. Which brings me to something I want to discuss with you. Come along to the living room. We'll talk about it there."

"Didn't I ought to clear the dishes?" Natty asked as they got up from the table. "Mrs. John said it would be nice if Mrs. Hollins found things tidy when she came in the morning."

Mr. Dunston was too surprised to comment on Natty's lapse in grammar; pantry details were of small significance in a busy lawyer's life. He quickly collected himself. "Yes, yes, of course," he ejaculated. "Quite right. You do that, Natty, and I'll get a fire going."

The fire was snapping briskly when Natty joined his father in the living room. "You've been a long time," Mr. Dunston remarked, uncritically for once.

"I know," Natty said. "But Mrs. John said it would be a good idea to rinse the dishes before I stacked them. So I did."

"All right," Mr. Dunston said. "What you did fits in with what I have in mind. You see, Natty, Mrs. Hollins isn't going to have Mother here to tell her how things should be done. It seems to me you could do that, up to a point, anyway. You know: how the table is set, the kind of things — simple things, of course — we like to eat. You could help her plan the meals and make lists of what we need from town. Groceries and so on."

"I couldn't do that!" Natty cried. The mere idea of telling Mrs. Hollins what she should do alarmed him; he couldn't possibly tell her how she ought to do it. She seemed to him a woman of very positive opinions. In her own house her word was law, just as much as his father's was here in their house and on the farm.

Some inkling of this may have occurred to Mr. Dunston, for he said, "Well, of course, you'd have to be tactful. But remember you'll be acting for me, so you have a perfect right to give orders."

Mr. Dunston sat down in his easy chair beside the fire and opened a book, as if he considered the matter settled, but Natty was far from reassured. He was still worried when it came time to bring his candle for his father to light, and Mr. Dunston apparently sensed his continuing disturbance.

"You must learn to ignore these fancies of yours," he said impatiently. "They'll get you nowhere in life. It's time you began to grow up."

But growing up was among the least of Natty's concerns as he reached the top of the stairs and started down the long hall to his room. For the first time, the full implications of Annie's going struck

home. He brushed his teeth as rapidly as possible — in fact, with just a right and left swish of the
toothbrush — and, candle in hand, made for his
room. As he passed the door at the head of the back
stairs, he became acutely conscious of Annie's
room at the foot, vacant now and lifeless. Though
he seldom saw her from the time they finished
supper until he went down for breakfast the next
morning, his awareness of her in the little room
below had been a reassurance. But from this point
on, he and his father would be alone with each
other until the time came to rejoin his mother and
sister in the city house. His father had become a
presence among the shadows that thronged outside
his door. He listened, holding his breath. But there
was nothing to be heard except the voice of the
brook. Then, as he got into bed, he did hear another sound. It had begun to rain, a patter on the
roof beyond his window that quickly turned into a
downpour — the kind of rain that came each September, eventually culminating in an equinoctial
storm.

As always, when he woke he was surprised to
find that he had been asleep. It was already growing light; the rain had stopped; but his room was
filled by the roaring of the brook. When he looked
out he saw that it had flooded into the meadow
above the driveway bridge. The water came down
the long granite slide with headlong urgency,

frothing and boiling in the pool by the corner of the house, then racing on full-voiced over the rapids beyond.

He was still standing at his window, bemused by the brook's turmoil, when the Hollinses' open buckboard drew up at the bridge to let Mrs. Hollins get down. It was a weather-beaten rig and their old horse Brown looked equally so. Instead of a top, Mr. Hollins had contrived one from a huge umbrella he had come across somewhere long ago; it was made up of alternating yellow and black panels advertising Gold Dust cleansing powder. Mrs. Hollins, in contrast, looked spritely and neat as she crossed the lawn to the kitchen steps. It was high time for Natty to dress.

When he entered the kitchen, he realized at once that it was now Mrs. Hollins's, just as before it had been Annie's. Though Mrs. Hollins gave him a pleasant good-morning, she had plainly marked out her boundaries, which, as nearly as Natty could make out, extended no farther than the door from the pantry into the dining room.

"I'd be glad, Natty," she said, "if you'd look at the table and see if there's anything I haven't put on."

He went to inspect, but the table looked all right to him. Mrs. Hollins gave a small, satisfied nod.

"I've fried some bacon and can poach an egg for your pa." Mr. Dunston invariably ate the same breakfast, only occasionally accepting a change on Sundays, if kidneys or chicken livers were available. "I know he likes oatmeal, but there isn't time today to get it for him. I'll cook up some this afternoon, though, and leave it in the double boiler for tomorrow."

This time it was Natty who nodded. "Maybe without oatmeal he'll want two eggs."

Mrs. Hollins agreed. "Maybe if you was to go and tell him it would be easier for him when he comes to sit down."

This struck Natty as a good suggestion and he went upstairs on his mission of diplomacy. He found his father nearly dressed and inclined to be reasonable, though he said it would have been perfectly simple for Mrs. John to have prepared his oatmeal yesterday afternoon. "But I suppose we ought not to expect her to know about such details."

To Natty's relief, breakfast went off affably. His father complimented Mrs. Hollins on her poached eggs and her cornbread and she acknowledged his approval with a reserved smile. She lacked Annie's chattering tendencies, which had often irritated Mr. Dunston. It was altogether an auspicious beginning of her tenure and Natty soon found that she was easier to be with than when in her own house.

But she remained as firm as ever in her attitude

about dogs. She would not allow Natty to bring Bingo into the kitchen as Annie sometimes had when she was sure Mr. Dunston was well away from the house. "Dogs," said Mrs. Hollins, "have their own place and they ought to have their own jobs to do and not just hang around as pets."

"Like Redskin," Natty observed.

"Yes. He's been a real good dog."

"Is he better?"

"No," Mrs. Hollins said. "And I don't expect he will be. Now that Bingo. He ought to be learning to get cows. Save a man going all the way up the flats. That would pay for the pup's feed."

"He's too young to do that," Natty protested.

"Foolish talk," Mrs. Hollins retorted. "Redskin wasn't six months old by the time he was fetching down our cows all on his own. It's better for a dog to have something hc knows how to do and have to do it. Better for a boy, too."

Natty chose to ignore that. He knew how strict she and Mr. Hollins were about Herschel doing his work and doing it right. But there was another side to her. She kept nice scraps for Bingo's bowl and even, when there wasn't enough, cooked up a fine-smelling mush of cornmeal with a little bran and gravy. And once he even saw her leaning over to pat the puppy as he wolfed his supper.

So a new pattern was established for living in the house that went smoothly enough. They worked out together what was to be for luncheon and supper and made out the shopping list for Jody to fill in town. Weekdays she served their supper in the dining room after lighting the candles on the table. Before that, too, she lighted the parlor lamp that stood on the writing table between the two front windows, for now, in September, the sun was setting earlier and on clouded evenings darkness came by half past six. But with the lamp lighted, Natty was able to look at one of the volumes of *Pictures from Punch* until his father came out of the living room.

Mr. Dunston himself seemed in a much easier frame of mind, partly due to his relief at their getting along so comfortably under Mrs. Hollins's ministrations. He even spoke approvingly of some dishes she liked to cook for her own family. "Cottage food," he remarked after they had left the table, "but tasty, quite tasty." His brief was progressing well, also; but mainly his good humor was due to a letter from Natty's mother that said she hoped to come up for a few days in the middle of the month, "to see how my two boys are getting along."

When they were together in the living room, with the fire going on the hearth, Natty's father made plans for what they would do to make her stay a happy one. "The partridge season will be open by then," Mr. Dunston said. "We can take long walks along the trails. I can go just ahead with my shotgun so if Major puts up a bird I might drop him for a special supper. I don't know if Mrs. Hollins will be equal to cooking a partridge, but she'll have your mother to tell her how."

Natty had thoughts of his own about how much pleasure his mother would get from such a program, but he kept them to himself. He had seen her other autumns returning from one of these "partridge walks," as Mr. Dunston called them, pale and tired-eyed, and sometimes he wondered if she had enjoyed their walk as much as she had assured his father she had.

But now there was another factor. When he and Bingo met Mr. Lewis next morning, the mailman said with obvious pleasure, "I have a letter addressed to you, Natty. I think it's from your mother."

It was. Usually she included a note to him in the envelope addressed to his father; and it occurred to him that she intended this one to be particularly for himself. Instead of opening it then and there, a premonition impelled him to put off reading it until he could be safe in his own room. The envelope would not fit into any of his pockets, so he stuffed it inside the front of his shirt. But then, realizing that its outline was visible there, he pushed it around until it rested at the small of his back.

"Nothing from Mother," commented Mr. Dunston. "Are you sure you didn't drop something on your way back?"

"No, I didn't," Natty replied. "But I'll go back down to make sure if you want me to."

Mr. Dunston's blue eyes regarded him fixedly, but then he glanced down at the large legal envelope from his office and started to open it. "We'll have lunch in a minute," he announced.

"I've got to go up and wash," Natty told him, and went. Upstairs, he fished the envelope out from his shirt but did not dare to take the time to look at it. Not until luncheon was over and his father had returned to his desk in the living room did he feel safe to open his mother's letter.

As he read, his heart filled with dismay, and cold fingers of fear began climbing his back. He had no idea of what he should do. What she wanted of him was far beyond his capacity and what little courage he was capable of. She wrote:

DEAR NATTY,

I have been so longingly looking forward to coming to be with you and Father for a few days, but it does not seem very likely now that I am going to be able to get away from here. Bessie has come down with another of those distressingly heavy colds she so often falls prey to, poor little mite. Of course I shan't think of leaving her here alone with the maids while she feels so miserably.

[57]

I haven't the heart yet to tell Father — his letters sound so eager about my coming to join "your two men," as he puts it. But I have been wondering if you might be able to break this bad news to him, perhaps a little at a time? Like perhaps saying you hope Bessie won't catch another of her colds? Father writes that you have been very helpful about advising Mrs. Hollins about the meals and the marketing. That leads me to hope you will find a way to make it easier for Father when he finds I can't come.

It did not help to have her end the letter with a message of "much love to my dear boy." For him to tell his father that anything he wanted so dearly to take place was not going to be was inconceivable. He simply did not have enough courage. As he sat staring blankly at the wall of his room, he tried to think what was best for him to do. Then a thought came out of nowhere. What if his mother were to write in a letter to his father that she had already told Natty she could not come and hoped he had given him her message? His father would want to know why he had not done so. He would also want to know when Natty got the letter from his mother. And there were no good answers. None at all. Though he had actually told no lie, Natty had allowed his father to think no letters had come this morning. To Mr. Dunston that would be the same as lying.

He could only hope that his mother would not

refer to the letter she had written him. But then another thought stole into his mind. In her own way his mother was as troubled as he about how his father would react. She would do whatever she could to deflect his anger. So she had turned to Natty, which to him did not seem fair, for she had put him in a position he saw no way of extricating himself from. He could not now tell his father about her letter. For an instant he thought of producing it tomorrow, as if it had only then reached him. But he saw that was not likely to work. His father had an unerring faculty for ferreting out misstatements. He would almost certainly ask Mr. Lewis if he remembered bringing Natty a letter from New York and Mr. Lewis would have no reason not to tell him. There was nothing Natty could do except wait for the lightning to strike.

When he got up from his chair, he became aware of an enormous tiredness. It was hard to get his legs to move, hard even to hold on to the letter. Perhaps that was because it seemed important to get rid of it. He considered tearing it up and flushing it down the toilet; but a stoppage earlier in the summer had resulted in direst threats. He dared not take the risk. He would have to dispose of it somewhere far off from the house. Once again he put it inside the back of his shirt and quietly went down the rear stairs.

Bingo, waiting outside the kitchen door, greeted

Natty with his usual jubilation. They went around the back of the house, avoiding the living room, and from habit rather than a sense of purpose headed towards the Hollinses' place. Instead of following the road, however, they took a path through the woods. It was one of a network of trails that Mr. Dunston had cleared each year for his own use during the bird-shooting season. Natty occasionally helped with the work — using a corn sickle, because he was not considered safe with an axe — and he was familiar with every bend and crossing. The path he and Bingo were now on led through a dense growth of evergreens. Even on a sunny day it was dark under the trees; the air was damp from running springs and sweet with balsam.

By this time Natty knew the place he was heading for. Where two logs carried the path over one of the largest springs, he turned left and followed the stream towards the river. As he neared the river road, the trees gave way to a tangle of alder and elderberry. The bushes grew so thick that, crawling under them, he and the puppy would be invisible to anyone passing along the road, which the spring passed under through a culvert.

Lying on his belly close against the rough stone arch, Natty fished out his mother's letter. He read it through once more, while Bingo watched him with an appearance of interest. Then Natty tore the letter into small pieces and began feeding them to the flowing water. As one by one they were sucked into the culvert, a sense of guilt grew in him, as if in committing the pieces of her letter to the spring he was in actuality destroying his mother herself. He watched the last bit float into the dark tunnel of the culvert and knew that something in his life had been irrevocably altered. He raised his eyes and saw Bingo still watching him. The puppy's tail hesitantly tapped the ground. Then both he and Natty were startled by a thud of hoofs and the rattle of wheels along the road just over their heads and Mr. Dunston's voice saying loudly, "I don't know where he is. He's always going off somewhere."

His voice rang out with exasperation. Whoever he was with made no reply, but it was probably Jody, who was sent over to Boonville most afternoons to pick up the late mail from New York at the Post Office. Once in a while Mr. Dunston liked to go along to clear his head, as he put it, after a day of wrestling with the law. Natty realized that there was no chance of getting back to the house before his father's return. Another black mark would be chalked against him on the list Mr. Dunston carried in his mind. It was a lugubrious walk home. Even Bingo, following for once on Natty's heels, seemed subdued.

His father was sitting on the front porch, a letter

in his hand. His blue eyes coldly watched the slow approach of his son, trailed by the nondescript brown puppy. In Mr. Dunston's mind both had the same hangdog look. His distaste was palpable in his voice.

"Where have you been?" he demanded.

"In the woods."

"What were you doing?"

"We went for a walk."

"Miles and miles." Mr. Dunston loaded the words with sarcasm. "Just walking and walking?"

"Not all the time," Natty said. "We stopped for a while."

"And what did you do when you stopped? Resting your weary selves, I suppose?"

"We were just seeing around," Natty answered, flushing. "Watching things."

"Brainwork," his father commented. "What did you watch?"

"Birds," his son said. "There was a chipmunk, and we watched the water."

"Watched water!" barked Mr. Dunston. "Don't you ever do anything worthwhile?"

"Sometimes," Natty said and realized instantly that if his father asked what, he wouldn't be able to give an answer, or at least one that his father would consider valid.

But Mr. Dunston's interest had shifted.

"Mother writes," he said, holding up the letter,

"that she won't be able to come after all," and Natty could tell from his voice how bitterly disappointed he was. He began to feel sorry for his father as well as for himself. But Mr. Dunston's voice again changed. "Mother says she hopes that maybe you had told me she might not be able to come. Did she write you?"

"Yes," Natty said. He was not sure that he had spoken out loud. But his father had heard him all right.

"When did you get the letter?"

"It came this morning."

His father's blue eyes held him in their chilling stare.

"You said there was nothing from Mother."

"*You* said that," Natty retorted. "And you asked me if I hadn't dropped something."

He saw the color deepen in his father's already flushed cheeks.

"You're impertinent." Mr. Dunston paused long enough to be sure Natty realized that. "I agree I did say it. But you allowed me to believe that there was nothing from Mother, and that's as bad as telling me a lie. What have you to say?"

Natty had nothing to say.

"So why did you allow me to believe there was no letter?

"Why?" repeated Mr. Dunston, raising his voice.

"I wanted to read it to myself first," Natty mumbled, aware of a growing numbness in his legs and arms.

"Perhaps I can understand that," Mr. Dunston said, as if he had made a great but unnecessary concession. "But when you did read it, why didn't you give me Mother's message?"

"It wasn't a message!" Natty creid out in desperation. "She asked me to tell you she couldn't come a little at a time so you wouldn't feel so ang— . . . so bad."

"Then why didn't you do that?"

"I didn't have time. Besides . . ."

"Besides?" Mr. Dunston demanded.

"I was afraid," Natty said simply.

"Afraid!" Mr. Dunston's voice vibrated with contempt. "What in God's name were you afraid of?"

"I was afraid you'd be angry."

"Is that any reason for not doing as Mother asked?"

Natty had no answer, and Mr. Dunston went on. "Apparently you are not only a liar but a coward."

His eyes bored into Natty's.

"Get out of here," he said. "Get out of my sight."

Natty went.

Not knowing what to do with himself, he went

to his own room and stood in the window looking out at the brook, losing his thoughts in the slide of water and engulfed in desolation. Obviously it would have been better to follow his mother's suggestion, but he told himself that there hadn't been enough time to think of the best way to tell his father. At the same time, however, a small thought began scratching a corner of his mind and after a few minutes he knew that a few more hours or even days between the arrivals of the two letters from his mother would have made no difference. He would never have dared give her message to his father. The run of the water seemed as endless as the dilemma he was now in.

But, as always happened on a farm, a distraction materialized to interrupt the ordinary rhythms of the place. Suddenly the sound of gravel being crunched into the drive was audible above the roar of the brook, and around the corner of the house appeared a scrawny pair of brown horses leaning desperately into their collars to drag an enormous steam engine behind them. It pulled so heavy on the ten-inch tires of its solid iron wheels that when it left the farm a second team hitched on ahead was needed to get it up the hill to Boyd's. But Mr. Dunston swore that it was the only one in the country powerful enough to run his mammoth Eureka corn through the silage cutter, so each fall he hired Framm's engine for the threshing as well as the corn cutting. During its stay activity on the farm reached a peak. It was a time that ordinarily Natty looked forward to with great excitement.

And now, as he turned from his window, he heard a second rig coming up the drive. It was the threshing machine itself — imposing, red, as big, he thought, as Noah's Ark. Forgetting his doubts and worries, he raced down the back stairs and across the brook to the barn to watch the process of setting up.

It was a ritual that never varied. In some way, incomprehensible to Natty, Lincoln John knew almost to the minute when the threshing machine would arrive, for he had the big gray team harnessed and waiting by the ramp that led up to the haymow floor. The grays stood impassively while Mr. Framm's exhausted horses hauled the great engine a short distance down the meadow road, leaving room for the threshing machine to make its turn at the foot of the ramp; but they pricked their ears when the thresher approached. They knew what they had been brought out for.

The horses hauling the heavy threshing machine stopped and the driver climbed down from the high seat. Natty knew who he was: Carney Flynn, a rough-spoken man who owned the third farm downriver from the Hollinses'. By what to Natty seemed immemorial rule, each farmer, when threshing ended on his place, supplied the team to take the machine on to its next assignment. Carney Flynn came over to the gray team and spat in front of their hoofs.

"What you bring them horses out for, Linc?" he asked. "Mine can take this thresher up into your barn just as good."

"Might be so," Lincoln John said quietly. "I'll help you unhook them, Carney."

Mr. Flynn's reply to that was one Natty could not have repeated to his mother or sister. He had tried quoting one of Mr. Flynn's remarks a year ago and had his mouth washed out in the laundry with brown carbolic soap. Lincoln John paid no attention to it either but went impassively about the business of hitching the gray horses to the thresher. "Want a ride up into the barn with me?" he asked.

He gave Natty a boost up and in an instant both of them were on the seat, looking straight down on the backs of the big horses. Lincoln John took up the reins and spoke a quiet word. The team moved as one, turning the threshing machine on its incongruously small wheels as easily, it seemed to Natty, as if it were a buckboard, and started up the ramp. Only the deep puckering of their dappled haunches gave any indication of the power they were putting into it. Actually, Natty supposed, it was no harder than bringing up one of the two-ton loads of hay, but seeing them from the seat of the high, red machine made it much more exciting. He would have liked to drive them in himself, but he knew better than to ask, though Lincoln John had allowed him to drive the horses in the hayfield while he and the hired hands were building a load on the big rack. Mr. Dunston, seeing his son one day on the top of the completed load, driving the horses towards the barn, had objected.

"He's too small to do that, Lincoln," he had said. "It's not safe. Those horses are too valuable to be driven by a child."

Mr. John had answered with his usual quiet. "Pshaw, Mr. Dunston. Natty can drive them as good as any man on this place and better than most. He knows them and they'll let him do anything he wants to them."

But Mr. Dunston angrily insisted and Lincoln John had had to take the reins. And now, just as the gray team's hoofs pounded on the planks of the mow floor and the front wheels of the threshing machine jerked over the sill, Natty caught a glimpse of his father at the edge of the ramp staring up at them. The gray horses bore back as one against the breechings and the machine stopped rolling, the end of the neap a comfortable yard short of the back wall. It was a neat, wholly controlled performance, which invariably filled Natty with wonder. The thing he wanted most in the world was for the day to come when Lincoln John

[*68*]

would say to him, "I wish you'd just drive the thresher up into the mow for me."

Instead Mr. John now said, quietly, "Maybe you better climb down and vamoose." Natty scrambled down, dropping the last few feet into the chaff on the mow floor. He could hear Lincoln John talking with his father on the other side of the machine.

"Yes, Mr. Dunston. He rode up on the machine with me."

"Did you let him drive the horses?"

"No. Not with the machine."

"Well, I disapprove anyway." Mr. Dunston's voice was tight and irascible. Natty did not wait to hear more. The stairs leading up from the milking floor were just beside him and he scuttled down them and went out between the long rows of stanchions to the door at the far end of the barn. He would have liked to watch while little Mr. Framm and his tall sons got the steam engine in place and adjusted the sixty-foot drive belt that reached up the ramp to the pulley on the thresher. But it seemed wiser to go back to the house, avoiding as long as possible his father's displeasure, which now appeared to pervade their life alone together in all its aspects, like an inescapable shadow. Now, entering the house, he seemed in his bewilderment to be walking into a darkening void.

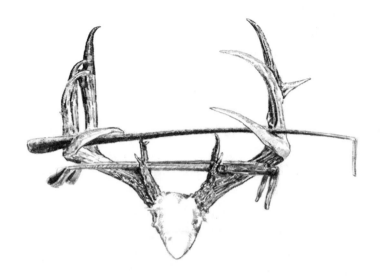

FOUR

❧ MRS. HOLLINS materialized at the pantry door, startling him because she had her bonnet, stiff with black ribbon, on her head.

"You aren't leaving, are you?"

A tremor in his voice made her look sharply at him.

"Yes," she said, nodding. "Carney Flynn's boy is coming with their buggy and he said they'd give me a ride home. I've laid out a cold supper for you and your pa. What's the matter?" she asked, looking searchingly at him again.

He dropped his eyes and said, "Nothing . . . I

don't know. It's only the house seems empty when you go."

She said impatiently, "Your pa's here, isn't he?"

Hoofbeats thumped the planks of the bridge.

"That's Flynn's boy now," Mrs. Hollins exclaimed. "I've got to get going."

She bustled out and a few minutes later Natty watched from the window as the Flynn buggy recrossed the bridge, Carney holding the reins, with his son and Mrs. Hollins crowded on the seat beside him and his team, hitched to a ring at the back of the box, trotting along behind.

He kept looking out of the window quite a while after they had gone. It was near sunset. Dark came earlier these days. He went into the pantry to see what Mrs. Hollins had laid out for their supper. Two plates covered with napkins, with quarters of cold chicken — breast for his father, second joint for himself. Mr. Dunston lived with the conviction that white meat was for adults, dark for children, and his convictions were tantamount to law. Natty wandered into the front hall and, seeing that the living-room door was open, went in to get one of the volumes of *Pictures from Punch* to look at while he waited for his father to come to supper. He left the book on the table between the parlor windows and went upstairs to bathe and change his clothes.

When he came down again, the house was already growing dark. In her hurry not to keep the Flynns waiting, Mrs. Hollins had neglected to light the lamps in the dining room and parlor, though she had left a light in the kitchen. It was too early to put their plates on the table, but as he looked at them he realized that he had not yet given Bingo his supper. He found the bowl of scraps Mrs. Hollins had left on the sink and took it out to the kitchen porch. Bingo was sitting at the top of the steps, dreamily staring at the slide of water in the brook. But the smell of his supper galvanized him. He wolfed it down and then danced around Natty all the way to the barn. There, however, he lapsed into a reluctant crawl that barely got him through the door of the stall that housed his kennel. He looked up with eyes grown tragic as Natty said good night over the door.

The farmhouse windows sent lights across the grass into the driveway, but walking home Natty kept in the shadow beyond their reach, as if impelled by a secret need to become invisible. It persisted even after he had entered the house; soundless as a ghost on sneakered feet, he passed through the lighted kitchen and pantry into the dining room, now nearly dark, past the living-room door, to the parlor. He opened the volume of *Pictures from Punch* and tried to make out the illustrations, but the pale sheen in the western sky, from which all color had now drained, was not enough. Familiar though he was with all the pictures, they were no more than blurred shadows on the paper. Then he noticed that the chair beside him did get some light from the window and he thought that if he sat in it with the book on his lap he might be able to look at a few of the drawings before the light faded completely.

Mr. Dunston had strictly forbidden his doing this but, crossing the bridge on his return from the barn, he had seen light in his father's bedroom window, indicating that Mr. Dunston was upstairs changing for supper. Natty thought he would have plenty of warning before his father came down, for Mr. Dunston's footfalls were as imperative as his voice.

As he balanced the book on his knees and opened it, he realized at once how easily it might bend too far, but he thought that by crossing his legs, with his right ankle just above the left knee, he could form a triangular base that would be safe; and it did, in fact, seem to work very well. Moreover, there was just enough light now falling on the page to allow him to identify, if not actually to discern, each illustration, and doing so brought him, as it always did, a feeling of reassurance and comfort. He had become utterly absorbed when he was made suddenly and chillingly aware of someone breathing.

Looking up, he saw his father.

"I thought I'd made it clear that you were not to open one of those *Punch*es except on a table."

The voice was low, almost calm, but to Natty's ears ominously vibrant.

"Can't you answer me?" asked Mr. Dunston in the same voice, now almost hushed. He was wearing his favorite pale tan homespun coat, with dark corduroy knickerbockers that had a sheen in lamplight, but now the whole figure looked gray and indistinct to Natty's alarmed eyes.

He barely managed to say, "Yes."

"Then why did you disobey me?"

"I needed something to do, to look at, while I was waiting," he explained. "It was too dark at the table."

"Couldn't you sit a few minutes without looking at something?"

Natty started to say no, but thought better of it. In the dark room they stared at the shapes of each other for a long moment. Then Mr. Dunston reached out his hands.

"Let me have the book."

He took it, still open. Natty sensed, rather than saw, the quivering of his father's hands. Then, deliberately, Mr. Dunston bent the covers back. The sound of the spine cracking seemed to reverberate between them.

"You see. You have broken it," Mr. Dunston said in a rising voice. "Just as I said you would."

"I didn't," Natty cried. "I didn't. You did it yourself."

"That's a lie and you know it. The book wouldn't have cracked if you hadn't broken it first."

It was not so much the illogic of what his father said as it was the cold relentlessness of his voice that overwhelmed Natty with terror and despair.

"I didn't break it," he said again, hardly hearing his own voice. If Mr. Dunston heard it, he was unmoved.

"You've lied to me too many times, Natty. In spite of warnings. This is the last time. I am going to teach you a lesson. Come into the living room."

He turned and walked briskly down the hall towards the lamplight shining from the living-room door. Natty, following on shaking legs, looked up to see his father's face as it came into the light. It was cold and set but flushed a fierce red, contrasting to his white, wiry hair, and Natty's desperately searching eyes could find no indication of a change of heart. He felt bewildered, not able to understand how matters could so suddenly have reached this frightful stage. He had disobeyed but he had not told a lie. He knew he had not.

Mr. Dunston walked over to the small sofa beneath the front window, over which were the deer horns and their assortment of riding crops and a small landing net that had been given to Natty's mother, but which she had never used. She was apt to rest on the sofa, waiting while her husband was upstairs changing for dinner. Often Natty joined her and they would look out together across the wide meadow. Sometimes they saw deer come out to graze in the twilight. But now the panes were black, reflecting his father and himself, and his mother was far off in New York City.

"Put down your trousers," Mr. Dunston commanded. "Your drawers too. It won't do you a bit of good to delay," he added as Natty's fingers fumbled at his belt buckle and fly buttons. He couldn't make his hands work properly. They did not seem to belong to him. He felt, in fact, as if he were two beings — the boy about to be punished and some other looking on. Both, however, heard his father say, "Bend over. You'd better lean your forearms on the sofa."

Leaning forward and down on the firm sofa seat, Natty did not dare look around at his father but stared instead at the reflected image in the window. He saw no sign of possible relenting there. The face seemed suddenly to have become cold, almost abstracted, as it looked down on the narrow presented buttocks. After a second this reflected image in the windowpane reached up one hand — towards the deer horns on the wall over Natty's head — and vanished from the glass. It seemed to hesitate a moment. Then it came once more into view, holding the South African quirt and Natty shouted, "No. Oh no!" Except that the shout was voiceless. His whole being along with his voice was paralyzed by dread. In total helplessness he saw the quirt raised shoulder-high. His father said hoarsely, "This will be a real lesson to you."

In the window Natty saw his father's hand start downward. He heard a sound between a whistle and a hiss and knew he had been hit, but for a moment he was aware of nothing but a swimming of his senses. His body felt locked in iron, completely numb, as if in agony there were no pain.

"By God," his father said. "That's not enough to make you even squeak?"

The quirt came down again and instantly pain broke through into Natty's mind. Every nerve he had was suddenly on fire. He had known nothing like it. He could conceive of nothing more awful. A scream tore from his mouth so wild and piercing that Mr. Dunston's head flung up like that of a startled horse. He realized that the window overlooking the drive and the bridge to the farm buildings was still open. He dropped the quirt and rushed to close it. As usual the wide sash offered difficulty, and while he struggled to shut it, Natty realized that this was his chance to get away.

His legs were quivering so badly that he did not know if he could stand, let alone get upstairs to his room. As he tried to straighten up, he became aware of having wet himself and the sofa as well; and then he saw that his bowels had also let go and left a pile of mess on the floor between his feet. He eyed it detachedly, for he was now being assailed by wave after wave of pain. He heard his father still wrestling with the stubborn window, and to his surprise found himself moving towards the door. Holding up his trousers, which had their own load of defecation, he passed along the hall and slowly climbed the stairs. He kept hearing little bleats of sound, which in the end he discovered were coming from himself.

To light his candle was unthinkably dangerous; he was in terror that his father might follow him upstairs. So, by touch, he felt his way to the bathroom and to the tub. Lifting his leg to climb into it set off fresh waves of pain, but after a minute they deadened a little and he let his pants and drawers fall. Steadying himself by holding on to a towel rack, he stepped out of them, then pried off his sneakers one after the other with the toes of the opposite foot. Still holding the towel rack by one hand, he washed himself with the other as well as he could in the dark. At the last moment, he thought of running some water into the tub for his clothes to soak in and to drown their reek. Then he groped his way into his bedroom, closed and bolted his door, and little by little, with infinite care, pulled on his pajamas.

Sleeping on his back or even on his side was out of the question, so he lay on his belly and for a long time tried to remember the exact order in which things had taken place. But pain and bewilderment blurred his thoughts; what had happened remained incomprehensible. The prospect of the day to come terrified him; beyond it he could not think at all. Yet after a while, mainly perhaps from utter nervous exhaustion, he fell asleep.

He woke slowly, reluctantly, his mind dazed. He was still lying on his belly and for a moment he thought that the pain had gone away. But the instant he stirred, it was with him, as fierce as it had been the night before. He lapsed again into immobility and tried to think of some less painful method of getting out of bed.

Lying inert, he became aware of a new sound audible above the roaring of the brook — something between a chug and a thump. It had a definite rhythm: three quick strokes followed by a much heavier fourth, repeated over and over — and suddenly he recognized the voice of Mr. Framm's old steam engine. Threshing had begun. It would continue until sundown, with only a half-hour break at noon. For a week, in one way or another, the life of everybody on the place would be keyed to the threshing machine and the engine that drove it, as though the wheezy thumping had become the very heartbeat of the farm. Natty knew that he ought to have been up long ago.

It was not that fact, however, so much as an abrupt awareness of having to get to the bathroom that nerved him to action. Still on his belly, he worked his legs out from under the covers and over the side of the bed, ending on his knees. The pain had not been unbearable, but when he started to climb to his feet he could not help crying out. Once he was erect, the pain lessened a bit and he managed to make his way into the bathroom.

It was not easy. In addition to the soreness in his buttocks, the muscles in all his lower body had stiffened, almost, it seemed to him, to the point of rigidity. He moved awkwardly, stick-legged, like a heron. Anyone, he realized with a crawling sense of shame, could tell that he had been whipped. He did not see how he could let himself be seen outside of the house. Yet he knew he would have to. Reluctantly, he started to untie the cord of his pajama bottoms, but the instant he tried to slip them off, the pain returned like a double tongue of flame. The bottoms seemed to have become stuck during the night.

As he stood there, trembling and wondering what to do, someone knocked at the bathroom door. He thought, for a terrifying moment, that it might be his father, and it took what little courage he had left to ask, "Who is it?"

"It's me," Mrs. Hollins said, opening the door and entering. To Natty's eyes, her face was without expression of any kind, and as she went on he could see no change even as she took in his problem with the pajama bottoms.

"Them ought to be soaked off. I'll get your sponge from the bathtub."

Natty tried to forestall her, but she was too quick. He did see, however, that the tub had been emptied and cleaned. Mrs. Hollins nodded briskly, as if she divined his question.

"I came up a while ago," she said, "when you didn't come down to get breakfast. I wasn't going to leave them clothes in the bathtub the way they was. They're washed out now and drying out back of the stove."

Natty could not bring himself to look at her again. He was appalled to think of what had been done about the mess he had left in the living room. It was impossible to visualize his father in the act of cleaning it up. The mere notion that he might even have attempted to do so was grotesque. Mr. Dunston had no inclination and still less talent for performing any task that seemed to him menial.

"Bend over," Mrs. Hollins told him, and the words sent a sudden chill through his heart. But she added matter-of-factly and quite kindly, "I've run the water warm so it hadn't ought to smart too bad."

For such a quick-moving woman and one so sharp-spoken in her own house, her touch was surprisingly light and deft. The warmth of the water was soothing; he was hardly conscious of the cloth loosening from his skin until his pajama bottoms fell around his feet and Mrs. Hollins commented, "Well. You've got a couple of hard welts there for sure. Stay like you are until I put some powder on them."

She dusted his buttocks liberally from a can of his little sister's baby powder and then said he could get dressed.

"I'll have some breakfast for you when you come down. I've fed your dog already."

The realization that he hadn't had a single thought for Bingo in all this time shamed him. It brought him close to tears and his voice faltered as he tried to thank her.

"Oh," she said. "Mr. John let him out from his pen and he reminded me himself when he came up on the porch."

She put away the powder, then stopped to pick up his pajama bottoms.

"I'll just wash these out," she said and added, as she left the bathroom, "Your pa's went out to the barn."

It took a minute or two for her meaning to get through to him. Then he saw that she thought it would be a good thing if he had his breakfast while

Mr. Dunston was still out watching the threshing. He dressed hurriedly and found a bowl of oatmeal porridge waiting for him on the kitchen table. He kept watch through the kitchen window as he ate, but his father did not come in sight, and he was upstairs again, looking out from his bedroom, when Mr. Dunston appeared, with his brisk, purposeful stride.

As Natty's father crossed the bridge, Bingo gave a tentative bark from the kitchen porch but was silenced immediately by Mr. Dunston's icy blue stare. Natty quickly drew back from the window for fear of his father's looking up. Mr. Dunston did, momentarily, but it was impossible to tell whether he had glimpsed his son, and he continued to walk on, turning the corner of the house towards the front door.

In a moment the front door slammed and Natty, going to his own bedroom door, opened it cautiously. He could hear his father in the hall below; then again the sharp closing of the front door. He went quickly to his bathroom and from its window saw Mr. Dunston walking down the drive with some letters in his hand. Natty did not know what to make of this action. Ordinarily his father would have shouted up the stairs, demanding to be informed why the mail hadn't gone and for Natty to come down instantly and take it. For him to have taken the letters himself without some expression of outrage was entirely out of character. Either, it seemed to Natty, his father was troubled by what had happened the night before or, in taking the letters down himself, he was laying up one more black mark against his son's deplorable record. It looked as if it would be a good idea to get out of the house for a while.

Waiting until his father had returned, Natty slipped down the back stairs, picked up Bingo, who cavorted in his usual ecstatic greeting, and went round the back of the house and down the brook shore to the fringe of woods that hid the river road from the house. There he and Bingo were safe from sight and he could walk at a less painful pace. Taking his time, he came out twenty minutes later on the top of the hill that faced the house. There, lying on his belly at the edge of a growth of brake-ferns, he could look down unseen over all the buildings.

The sun, climbing the sky towards noon, had become, as it often did in early September, almost summer-hot. Even under the brakes, Natty could feel its warmth, comforting to the soreness of his buttocks. The perspective made everything seem small in relation to himself. The pond on his left shone like brass and the brook threading the pasture and meadows below it glittered on its rapids. On either bank the gray buildings were toy blocks arranged by a child's hand. The roar of the threshing machine was barely audible; even the wheeze and thump of Mr. Framm's engine was muffled by distance.

Faint though it was, the persistent beat became almost hypnotic, and gradually Natty's thoughts drifted into fantasies. The whispery sound of the steam engine became the thudding of war drums and Natty himself the scout guiding a wagon train through hostile Indian country. The buildings had become lodges, and safe passage for the wagons could only be assured by picking off the big white chief. While he watched, Natty saw his father come out onto the front porch in his white hat and knickerbockers. In imagination Natty felt beside him for his buffalo rifle, aimed, and pressed gently on the trigger. As the black powder-smoke from the discharge cleared, he saw his father come down the porch steps — not, of course, the Indian chief; but Natty in his heart realized with chilled suddenness that it was his father at whom he had aimed.

He flattened himself still farther under the brakes and watched his father walk rapidly down the drive and after a few minutes reappear with a bundle of mail in his hand. Before entering the house, Mr. Dunston paused and looked out across the front meadow. To Natty it seemed that his father was staring straight at his hiding place. He hissed at Bingo to lie down and his voice was so desperate and urgent that, unexpectedly, the puppy obeyed. Mr. Dunston stayed a moment longer searching the hill before turning to enter the house. It was evident that he had seen neither the puppy nor his son.

Natty let out a long breath of relief, and Bingo, sensing the changed atmosphere, bounded to his feet and went off in search of anything that scurried or jumped. Watching drowsily, Natty lay inert as a lizard. He might have drifted off to sleep but for a sudden stillness. The thump of Mr. Framm's engine had ceased, which meant that it was noon and the hired hands would be laying off for lunch.

They ate at a table made up of long planks resting on sawhorses on the lawn in front of the farmhouse porch. On it Mrs. John, with a couple of women helping her, laid out plates of thick sandwiches. Natty considered Mrs. John's sandwiches of cold pork with a little dark brown gravy on them the best in the world, and she had always let him have one or two until Mr. Dunston heard of it. He did not approve a member of his family's mingling with the threshing crew. They were apt to use profanity; one or two of them were positively foulmouthed.

"And in any event, Natty, it's not right to take food intended for laboring men. You have your own here at home."

This seemed to Natty a specious argument, considering the mountains of sandwiches and the number of pies of all sorts Mrs. John and her helpers had provided. But in any case, he was not going to have one of her pork sandwiches today. Nor had he any intention of joining his father at lunch in the big house. He would stay up on the hill and if people were worried by his absence, let them worry.

About half an hour later, he saw the men walking in twos and threes towards the barn. The thump of the steam engine began, hesitant at first, but soon regaining its rhythm. The faint whirring of the belts on the thresher pulleys grew into a roar as all parts of the machine came into play, and suddenly from the mow door the cloud of dust and chaff rolled out, climbing steadily until it towered high above the roof. Dreamily gazing down from his hilltop, Natty felt himself removed from all the busy hustle of the farm, as if he himself were an observer from another sphere. All sound faded away. He lay entranced, safe from threats and dangers, unaware of the passage of time until, for no discernible reason, the noise of the threshing returned. He saw that the shadows of the trees had stretched eastward across the meadows, and he realized that sooner or later he would have to return to the house and face his father.

FIVE

✿ MRS. HOLLINS was beginning to get supper when Natty came in from the kitchen porch.

"Do you calculate to eat downstairs, Natty? Or will I fix you a plate to take up?"

"Downstairs," he mumbled, and was surprised, when she asked him to repeat, that he had said it. The decision to come back to the house and encounter his father, he now saw, had been no more than part of his hilltop fantasies, stemming from the sight of his father's figure made tiny by the long downward perspective. But the suspicion that Mrs. Hollins had heard him clearly seemed to him to leave no alternative, and he said more loudly, "I'll come down for supper."

"That would be best, I think," Mrs. Hollins said, with what Natty took to be an approving nod. "You go upstairs now and I'll give Bingo his supper."

Her tone of voice encouraged him to ask how Redskin was getting along.

"About the same," she said. "He don't seem to get any better. I don't guess he ever will, being he's so old a dog. But he don't seem much worse off, either. My brother said he'd ought to have been shot long ago. Put him out of the pain of dying, was what he said. But Mr. Hollins said no. Redskin's been in the family so long he could be allowed to die on his own time."

She picked up Bingo's dish, added a little brown gravy to it from a saucepan on the stove, and said over her shoulder as she started for the door, "If you want some help, just holler down the stairs."

Natty thanked her; but he didn't think he would and, as it turned out, he did not. He used his sponge, as Mrs. Hollins had in the morning, to soak off his drawers and took a kneeling bath in his tub. Then, with a palm full of his sister's powder, he patted down his buttocks, using the swollen welts to guide his hand. They hurt when he touched them but not more than he could bear, and he preferred doing it himself to having Mrs.

Hollins's help. He wondered, though, how he was going to sit through the whole supper. After he had dressed, he tried sitting on his bedroom chair, and he decided that if he leaned slightly forward, he might get through the meal.

In the kitchen, Mrs. Hollins reported that Bingo had finished his supper and that Mr. Dunston had come back to the house after spending some time at the threshing. Natty looked sharp at her; it seemed to him that her mind ran on the same track as his, but she had turned back to the stove and her face, wreathed in the pleasant vapors of her cooking, told him nothing. So he went out to put Bingo in his kennel for the night. Bingo put on his usual act of wistful sadness, and as Natty looked over the stall door, an uneasy notion entered his head that the puppy did not really belong to him and never had, whatever his mother's intention.

Mrs. Hollins had set the dining-room table by the time he came back to the house. She was not leaving early tonight, she told him as she picked up the black iron kettle to refill it. (Natty noticed that she seemed to like having a dish or utensil in her hand whenever she had something special to say.) Mr. Hollins was coming to pick her up around eight, when she would have finished clearing up after their meal. How, during the day, she had managed to make this arrangement, Natty had no idea. But it brought him a little reassurance, and he finally worked up enough nerve to go into the front of the house.

Tonight the lamps in the dining room and parlor had been lighted, and as he passed the living-room door, he saw that the lamps there also were lit but the room was empty. Evidently Mr. Dunston was upstairs getting ready for supper. For the moment, at least, Natty had nothing to be afraid of. But he had no inclination to take out one of the volumes of *Punch*. He never wanted to touch them again.

Through the front window of the parlor, he watched the twilight fade until the meadow lost all outlines and the dark began to press against the windowpanes and his reflection stared in at himself. At the sight of that pale and narrow face, he felt the small amount of resolution he had managed to collect begin to dissolve, and as a distraction he turned to one of the glass-fronted bookcases. The lower shelf was stocked with bulky volumes such as *The Home Book of Verse*, which was filled with what seemed to Natty uninteresting poems, but the upper shelves carried rows of white, paperbound books that he had never looked at. Now, on the spine of one, his eye was caught by a name he recognized: R. L. Stevenson, whose *Treasure Island* their mother had read aloud to George and himself the previous summer. This book was called *The Strange Case of Dr. Jekyll and Mr.*

Hyde, and Natty opened it tentatively. But the opening page dealt with an elderly lawyer in London, a rather forbidding individual with a fondness for gin and good wine: "lean, long, dusty, dreary, and yet somehow loveable," a man who sometimes wondered at the misdeeds of his friends but was "in any extremity inclined to help rather than reprove." This person, named Utterson, immediately appealed to Natty, and he was to read the story with much more interest in and concern for the dry old lawyer than for the unfortunate physician who was ostensibly its hero.

However, before he could turn to the second page, he heard his father's step at the foot of the stairs. There was no time to restore the book to its shelf as he might have done; Mr. Dunston spotted it at once and demanded to see what he was reading.

"Pretty sensational stuff for a boy your age," he pronounced. "Lurid, as a matter of fact." He gave the book a shake, as a terrier might shake a rat already dead. "Still, it might show you how depravity of any kind leads itself on to eventual disaster. You may read it, if you like."

Natty muttered that he would like, which made his father tell him not to mumble and in the same breath declare that they should not keep Mrs. Hollins waiting any longer, though Natty could not see how he himself had been responsible for keeping Mrs. Hollins waiting at all. But the meal passed more easily than he could have foreseen.

It was evident that Mrs. Hollins had taken extra pains and come up with one of Mr. Dunston's favorite dishes: lamb's liver very thinly sliced and sautéed with onions. He complimented her on it and for the rest of the meal as well. After going without lunch, Natty appreciated the food as much as his father, if not in quite the same way. Mrs. Hollins beamed with satisfaction as she took out their empty plates, and Mr. Dunston became almost chatty, for the most part about how the threshing had gone. At one point he nonplussed Natty by asking his opinion on a matter over which he had disagreed with Lincoln John, a question Natty had sense enough to evade by saying that he did not know. If his son's declining to take his side nettled him, Mr. Dunston did not show it. Instead he praised Mrs. Hollins for the dessert she had elected to give them, and this mood of general satisfaction carried over to their adjournment to the living room.

Mr. Dunston threw another log on the fire and sat down in his accustomed chair to one side of the hearth, crossing his legs so that the fancy pattern in the cuffs of his golf stockings showed to best advantage. The stockings were a pair that Natty had particularly admired and perhaps Mr. Dunston had counted on the fact, for he said, "I am going to propose a job for you to carry through the last month of our stay on the farm. I don't think you will find it onerous, Natty. If you apply yourself intelligently to it, you should find it interesting and rewarding."

"How do you mean, 'rewarding'?" Natty asked, with a faint hope that money was involved.

His father visibly stiffened. "I don't think, in view of our relations at present, that it is appropriate for you to ask for money. I mean rewarding," he went on, "in the sense of your own satisfaction in carrying out a useful task."

Somewhat bewildered, Natty raised his eyes to find his father watching him with a cool, equivocal smile. His innate cautiousness was instantly awakened. But before he could think of anything to say, Mr. Dunston explained: "What I want you to do is to keep a game record for me. The bird season opens tomorrow and I plan to take time off most afternoons with Major."

Major was Mr. Dunston's old black cocker spaniel who lived alone in a fenced yard up the brook and out of sight behind the stone smokehouse. Until the hunting season opened, except occasionally for Sunday walks, he seemed to Natty a nonentity, disregarded, forgotten, whose only excitement was a distant sight of someone passing by to be greeted with hysterical barking. But Mr. Dunston had an iron conviction that hunting dogs should be kept strictly apart from human domestic life and never share in demonstrations of affection.

"Hunting dogs are for hunting," he often declared. "And for hunting only. It keeps them keen."

Now he went to his desk and returned with a small Leatherette notebook, which he handed to Natty before sitting down in his chair.

"I got this in Boonville for you to keep the record in," he told Natty. "It's big enough so you can get one day's report on two pages. Each page you turn will be for the next day. I suggest you put the date of each day at the top of the left-hand page. You'd better mark all the pages now, to begin with. That will give you something worthwhile to do."

"But if you don't go out or don't shoot a bird?" Natty asked. "Do I leave the page blank?"

"No," Mr. Dunston said. "You should say I could not get off to go shooting. Or if I get nothing, say that. Put down the birds I saw but had no chance at. And then for every day, what the weather was like. Cold, rainy, sunny, windy . . ."

Natty looked down at the book with a creeping distaste. Also with a kind of fear. As if it were a loaded gun pointing at him.

"I guess," he said after a minute, "what you want is a list of everything you kill. Would I put down rabbits, too?"

As soon as he uttered the words, Natty realized he had made a mistake. His father had stiffened; Mr. Dunston's face grew redder. The intake of his breath before he spoke was harsh.

"Are you implying that I am going out to murder living creatures? They're game. Grouse and woodcock have a much better chance of getting away than I have of hitting them. And anyway, you don't 'kill' them, you 'bag' them, just as you don't say 'rabbits' when what you are after is a varying hare." He paused and after another rough breath said icily, "You had better go upstairs now, and before you go to bed you had better date the pages as I told you. So you can show them to me in the morning."

Natty left with a sense of having been reprieved, but as he reached the door, his father called him back.

"You haven't brought your candle to be lighted. Nor have you said good night." Words in judgment that brought a sense of sudden cold.

But they went through the usual motions, stiffly as though they had been mechanized. Natty's good-night was hardly audible, even to himself.

He followed his candlelight up the stairs and along the hall to his bedroom, placed the candlestick on his desk, and, after bolting his door, got his matches out of their hiding place. Then he blew out the candle and relighted it himself. Sitting down at the desk, he took up the penholder and dipped the stub pen in the inkwell. Merely to touch the notebook repelled him, which may have caused his unformed writing to look even more scrawly than usual. But he had no doubt that there would be some sort of reckoning if he did not have all the pages dated to show his father in the morning.

"Did you date the pages of the game record the way I told you?" Mr. Dunston asked at breakfast.

"Yes," Natty said. "Do you want to see it?"

But Mr. Dunston seemed to have other things on his mind and did not answer. Immediately after lunch he went out to view the threshing. Two hours later, Natty, in his bedroom, heard a series of wild canine hallelujahs up the brook and from his window saw Major, a black projectile streaking over the meadow for the woods. His father followed, with a shotgun cradled in his left arm and his right hand at his mouth as he blew fiercely on his dog whistle — which Major, if he heard it, plainly chose to ignore.

SIX

IT WAS another warm, windless afternoon, too warm, Mr. Dunston had said, really to think of going hunting. Too many leaves were still on the trees. The woods were so dry it would be impossible to move quietly. All the odds, he had emphasized to Natty, were against his bagging a bird. He was going, as a matter of fact, only for the sake of a walk and to give Major a run at last.

Natty hurried down the hall to the front window and watched his father until he had crossed the meadow and disappeared into the woods. Major, of course, had long since vanished; but presently Natty heard his voice raised in shrill, sustained barks that faded into nothing and he knew that the spaniel must, to his own utterable joy and Mr. Dunston's exasperation, be hot in pursuit of a rabbit. Knowing that temporarily he had the house to himself, Natty went down to the parlor to get *The Strange Case of Dr. Jekyll and Mr. Hyde,* took it up to his room, and, lying belly down on his bed, began to read with growing absorption the story of a man who chose deliberately to cultivate the baser human instincts that lead to evil.

A distant shot brought him back temporarily to the present and himself in his bedroom. He recognized the report of his father's Sauer gun. Mr. Dunston had had the barrels shortened for snap shooting at woodcock in the alder bottoms; it had a harsh, flat sound, like the bark of an angry dog — very different from the report of the longer-barreled Webley or his brother George's single-barrel Stevens. After wondering for a moment whether his father had fired at a partridge or a rabbit, he returned to his reading. There were one or two shots at intervals after that, but in his absorption he hardly heard them and it was only the slamming of the front door that finally recalled him from Mr. Utterson's London. Mr. Dunston had returned from the woods.

A minute or two later Natty heard his father's

voice talking to Mrs. Hollins in the kitchen. "Just one," he said to her. "A hen partridge, rather small. Possibly a this-year's bird."

Mrs. Hollins's voice replied, but her words were indistinguishable. Natty realized he had better get downstairs. It was time to give Bingo his supper and take him out to bed in the barn. His father would not like Bingo around while Major was out of his yard. But by the time he had bathed for supper and changed his shirt, Major had been taken out to his kennel with his supper; Mr. Dunston had gone up to his room to change, and the coast was free.

"He seems to have enjoyed himself," Mrs. Hollins observed. "He must have missed some shots, but he got this little partridge and that makes all the difference."

Natty stroked the feathers, seeing the varied markings of brown and gray. It seemed to him that the body still had warmth. On one side of the head, just below the eye, was a droplet of blood. Mrs. Hollins noticed the way he looked at it.

"Must have been a shot did that. Likely the shot was scattered, which means she was pretty far away from your pa when he fired." She was making a loop of string, and now she fastened it around the bird's neck, handed the end of the loop to Natty, and told him, "You might just take this to the icehouse and hang it on a hook in the meat room when you're taking Bingo out to the barn."

Bingo was enthusiastically curious about the partridge, jumping with little yelps of excitement. Natty finally lowered the bird within the puppy's reach, with a precautionary hand on his neck. But even so, Bingo managed to catch hold of a leg and Natty had some difficulty making him let go; they crossed the bridge to the icehouse with the young dog cavorting around the boy and the bird as if celebrating a triumph all of his own doing.

With the sun near setting, there was little light inside the cold meat room. Natty could barely make out the split carcasses of two lambs and a pig on one side and a row of fresh-killed chickens on the other. Obviously that was where the partridge belonged, and Natty slipped the loop over one of the meat hooks. He had been surprised by the light weight of the bird, suspended from his index finger; now the slim feathered form looked to him pathetic and lonely next to the solid, clean-picked bodies of the chickens, headless and hung by their feet. It was a relief to swing the heavy door shut and move on with Bingo to the barn.

The threshers had finished for the day and gone home. The farmhands were bringing in the herd. The cows filed down the runway, dividing right and left to their allotted places, and Lincoln John came down one row closing the stanchions.

"Hello," he said. "We missed you today. Didn't see you yesterday, when it comes to that."

"No," Natty said. "I stayed in." He realized that was not exactly true, but it was not exactly lying, either. However, Lincoln John's face gave no indication of knowing that anything had happened to Natty. He merely smiled his slow smile and said, "Hope you'll be out tomorrow. We ought to finish threshing before supper. If not, Saturday noon by latest."

"I'll be out," Natty answered him. For some reason, he felt immensely better after this exchange, as if the gears of his life were falling into mesh again. But passing the icehouse made him think once more of the dark feathered body alongside the chickens, and when he entered the kitchen he asked Mrs. Hollins right away why the partridge had to hang by her neck when with the chickens it was just the opposite.

"Is it because she's wild?" he asked.

"Maybe partway that's why," she said. "It's because to gentlemen like your pa wild birds or deer meat taste better strong. Your pa calls it 'gamey.' They keep a bird ten days or two weeks before they eat it. Deer meat even longer."

"But why does she have to hang from her neck?" Natty persisted.

"Because that helps to bring the gamey taste," Mrs. Hollins replied. Natty felt that she was not too sure of her reasons but, like unsure people, she felt obliged to be factual. "You'll have noticed," she said, "we didn't pick the feathers off *nor* did we draw the bird's innards. It has to stay that way to bring up the wild, gamey taste."

"But they hang the chickens upside down," Natty said.

"They've been picked and drawn, that's why." Mrs. Hollins's voice was slightly tart, as if she was getting tired of the discussion. But suddenly her eyes brightened. "Mr. Dunston told me why. If you hang the partridge by the neck, then the innards will drop down instead of laying against the breast. It's the breast meat is the best and your pa don't want it tainted when the innards get too strong." She looked straight at Natty, almost triumphantly.

Dutifully, he said, "I see," and went out into the parlor, just in time to meet his father as he reached the foot of the stairs. They went right in to the dining table and as soon as they had sat down, Mr. Dunston rang the little handbell, greeting Mrs. Hollins with a word of praise for the lamb broth before he even tasted it.

He was evidently in a good mood. As they ate he gave Natty a highly circumstantial account of his afternoon. He had followed the river woods —

Major, like a lunatic, putting up birds too far ahead even to glimpse, let alone shoot at — and the woods were so dry that even when he, himself, took a separate course from the dog's, the birds heard him before he had a proper chance to shoot. It was truly frustrating, and it was not until four o'clock that Major so much as gave a thought as to why they were out together and came in search of him. The wooly black imp rushed up behind him, tongue hanging out a mile, his ears tangled with twigs and dodder vine. A less amiable man would have cut a stick and beaten him; instead he sat down on a log and they shared a bar of chocolate. After that Major hunted with a reasonable regard for his master's whereabouts. It showed, really, how patience and a little understanding sometimes had better results than rigid discipline. Near five o'clock, when it was beginning to get shadowy in the woods, Major put up a bird that broke diagonally towards Mr. Dunston.

"A quartering shot head-on," he explained to his son. "Quite a way off. Very difficult. Someone less alert would have missed it. I was fortunate at that," he finished modestly, but with a degree of complacency too. "Did you see the bird?"

"Yes," Natty told him. "I took it out to the ice-house and hung it up alongside the chickens."

His father was looking at him in a way that made him think more was expected of him; he couldn't think what. So he added, "I thought she was pretty."

"What made you think is was a female?"

"I heard you tell Mrs. Hollins it was a hen bird," Natty said. "But she looked to me like a girl partridge. I guess that's why I thought she was pretty."

"You feel it's only female creatures that are pretty?" asked Mr. Dunston. "Don't you think males are?"

"No," Natty said.

"What do you think they are, if not pretty?"

"I don't know."

"Handsome, maybe?" Mr. Dunston asked.

"I guess so. Some, maybe."

He was afraid his father might ask what Natty thought of him. He knew his father was strikingly good-looking; other people said that; but he felt a sudden, crawling reluctance to say so. Finally he said, "Bulls aren't handsome. But I think some cows are pretty."

He thought he could see an expression of dislike come into his father's face. He added, "Bulls are big. They're scary. Rustum's eyes get hot when they look at you through the bars."

"You are mostly afraid of things, aren't you?" his father said. He dabbed his mouth with his napkin. "We'd better go in the living room so Mrs. Hollins can clear up."

Seated by the fire, Mr. Dunston went on with his detailed account of his afternoon until Natty nearly dozed off. But he was suddenly jerked back to his senses by his father demanding to know what he was going to write as the day's entry in the game record.

For an instant thoughts whirled without form through his mind. Then, drawing an uncertain breath, he began.

"A hot day, bright sun, and south wind. Father had only a few shots, very long, and missed until Major came back to him and they had some chocolate. Then Major hunted closer. He put up a bird off to Father's left and it came quartering back. A very hard shot to make, but Father dropped the partridge and bagged it. No other bird, or shots either."

Natty had surprised himself by being able to say so much and Mr. Dunston was not unimpressed. He said, "That's quite good. Put it down the way you said it and it will make a good entry to start off the record."

His father's approval came so infrequently that Natty was more startled than reassured. In addition, his intuition told him that Mr. Dunston's approving tone had as much to do with his own shooting as his son's description of it. When, later, they went through the ritual of lighting Natty's candle and Mr. Dunston said, "You'd better write that entry in the game book before you forget," Natty nodded, not wanting to answer in words. Climbing the stairs, he felt increasingly uneasy without knowing why. It was only after he had bolted his bedroom door that he realized that he wasn't going to write down the record of his father's afternoon and the lone partridge whose shooting seemed to mean so much to him. He told himself that he would just put it off until next morning; he could as easily remember what to write then as he could tonight. But when he stopped at his desk and fingered the notebook, he experienced a revulsion so powerful as to be almost nauseating and he knew then, without having to acknowledge it to himself, that he was not going to write down anything at all about his father's hunting.

He did not fall asleep at once, as almost always happened; and when he finally did sleep, it was restlessly, with extravagant dreams, about which he remembered nothing when he woke a little after daybreak, except that he had been frightened. After putting on his clothes, he went over to the desk and looked down at the notebook. He did not pick it up or even touch it. He tried to fool himself by thinking that he would come up after breakfast and put down the details of his father's afternoon, but in his heart he did not believe that. When during breakfast Mr. Dunston asked whether he had

made the entry in the game record, he said he had,
looking straight back at his father's eyes and realizing he was telling a conscious and deliberate lie.

Mr. Dunston did not pursue the subject. Either
his mind was peoccupied by his legal work or,
more likely, by the threshing, for as soon as he had
finished breakfast, he went out to find Lincoln
John. As he watched his father leave, Natty sub-
sided into a state of panic and relief as he thought
of what might have happened if he had been asked
to produce the game book. He went upstairs with
the uncertain intention of this time entering yesterday's record; but once again he could not bring
himself to touch the book. He stared at the pen on
its tray, at the inkwell with its brass cupola top,
but he did nothing; and after a few minutes he
turned away bewildered and numb, and went
quietly down the back stairs and out across the
brook, hardly seeing where he walked. He did not
come to himself until he felt Mr. John's hand drop
on his shoulder and heard him saying in his quiet
voice, "I'm glad you came out. We ought to finish
threshing about noon and I was thinking if you'd
come along when we hauled Framm's engine over
to Boyd's, you and me could ride the gray team
home. You on Kit and me on Charlie. Or the other
way around if you'd rather do it that way."

The times Natty felt best were when he was
able to join Lincoln John in some farm activity, but

riding the gray team back from Boyd's would be a special treat. He said eagerly that he would like to and went back to the house to ask permission. His father said he could go if it did not interfere with his getting the mail, but he added it was a pity Natty could not find something really useful to do.

"But it *is* useful," cried Natty. "Getting Kit and Charlie home again."

"I suppose it hasn't occurred to you that Lincoln John could bring the horses back perfectly well without your help," Mr. Dunston observed.

"But it wouldn't be the same."

Natty was leaving the room as he said this and realized at once that he would have been smarter to have held his tongue. At least he wasn't called back. He said a wordless prayer that Mr. Lewis would not be late with the mail, for if he was, Mr. John might be obliged to start for Boyd's before Natty could get back with the letters.

He went down the river road well before the usual time, listening impatiently for the sound of Benjamin's hoofs on the bridge planks. Up by the barn Mr. Framm's engine went thudding on as if it never planned to stop. In the low willow bushes along the brook, Bingo prospected for green frogs, his tail stiff with elation whenever he got one to jump into the water. Natty became so absorbed in Bingo's game that he almost missed the rattle of the planks on the river bridge. Then, as he watched the old white horse trotting down the road, the bitter realization came to him that he wouldn't be able to ride Kit home from Boyd's. It had been as much as he could manage to sit on the edge of the chair at meals. He would have to tell Mr. John, though he did not see how he could explain why.

Now he would have been glad to waste time talking to Mr. Lewis, enough time so that Lincoln John would have to leave without him; but this day Mr. Lewis seemed anxious to get on. The thumping of the steam engine continued undiminished as Natty made his way back to the house. Noon was at hand when he took the letters for the farmhouse across the brook, and it was now evident that the men would not be taking the threshing machinery over to Boyd's until after lunch. So he would have to tell Mr. John he could not go with him after all.

SEVEN

"WELL, now. I'm sorry to hear that," Mr. John said, looking down at Natty. "You ain't feeling good?"

"I feel all right," Natty told him. "But I hurt. To sit on a chair. It would be worse on Kit." He looked upward into Lincoln John's mild eyes and saw only concern in them. "My father whipped me." He hadn't meant to say that; he didn't know what impelled him to tell Mr. John. He felt suddenly frightened and insecure.

"Well, now," Mr. John said mildly. "What did he do that for?"

"He said I lied to him. But I didn't lie. He hit me with the African quirt, the one you helped me fix."

Mr. John looked at him without expression of any kind.

"That sounds pretty hard," he commented after a moment. "Maybe you done something else that got him mad."

"I was holding a book on my lap when he'd told me I could only read it if I laid it on a table."

"That still sounds pretty hard," Mr. John said slowly. "Might have been because of something you didn't do."

Natty could hear the question in his voice, but he didn't see how he could tell about his mother's letter. Lincoln John paused, but when he saw that Natty had nothing to say he went on: "Men get mad in different ways. But what I've seen in my time, most get mad because they've got scared. You'd do best to try and forget it, Natty. It's over now anyway."

Natty did not reply. He wasn't sure at all that it was over. In fact, in his bones he knew that it was not. He did not want to dispute with Mr. John, whose face was still full of concern and kindness.

"I'll tell you what," he said. "Why don't you come over with us as far as the canal bridge and wait while we go up Boyd's lane to the barn? I'll be walking back of the horses and you can walk along with me. Then I'll come back with Kit and

Charlie and I can hoist you up on Kit. She's got a nice round back. I doubt she'd hurt for you to sit on as much as a chair would, and she and Charlie'll be just walking. But if it hurts too bad, say so and I'll take you off. We'll just walk home together and nobody will be the wiser."

Looking up into Mr. John's face, Natty felt his heart flood with warmth. "Yes," he said. "I'll come."

"Better get a sandwich from Mrs. Hollins, because we'll be starting before your pa would want his lunch."

Natty ate the sandwich sitting at one side of the haymow door with Bingo at his feet, both of them gazing over the meadow towards Boyd's. He gave the last corner of the sandwich to Bingo, who devoured it with appreciative gusto just as Mr. John appeared with Kit and Charlie around the corner of the barn. Behind him came the teamster, Benson, with the bay second team, and after them the Framm sons with their scrawny pair. Departure from the barn followed a set routine — Natty had watched it other times and knew what to expect.

It had been established by Lincoln John the summer the big gray team had come to the farm. First he brought the grays up onto the mow floor, leading Kit and carrying the neck-yoke in his free hand. For all her size, Kit was very feminine and liked to play cute so that people would pet her and give her sugar or a carrot; but Charlie, as Mr. John said, was a straight, honest horse, just as kind and more patient. Natty loved both of them and they would let him do anything — pass under their bellies in their stalls, or even drink between them at the watering trough, with his hands on each throat to feel the balls of water going down. They were half Percheron, Mr. John said, and a lot more horse than he had seen in any team all his life.

They backed the towering threshing machine out of the haymow floor and down the ramp with its vertical wall on each side, a step at a time, never allowing the slow pace of wheels to alter even when they pitched off the level planking onto the steep ramp. At its foot they cramped the front wheels to turn it until the neap was pointed down the meadow road, and during this performance, Lincoln John held the reins loose, saying a quiet word now and then. He called it talking them down, and he would not allow any other hand or team to back so valuable a machine out of his barn.

The gray team was unhooked from the threshing machine and the bay second team took it over. Tom and Nellie were stocky, strong horses, but nervy compared to Kit and Charlie. They led the procession. Then came the steam engine, its broad iron wheel-rims grinding on the gravel spots, hauled by Framm's scrawny team, with Kit and Charlie ahead of them, their evener hooked into the iron loop on the engine's neap. With the four horses pulling, it went right along. One of the Framm boys rode on the seat of the engine; Lincoln John with Natty walked on the edge of the road just behind the gray team, while Bingo raced forward to lead the threshing machine, then came bolting back to supervise the engine.

"It looks to me," Mr. John said in an amused voice, "as if that Bingo of yours has the makings of a cowdog. Leastways, he thinks he has."

The pup raced back to the front, where the threshing machine was making the turn to the river bridge. Benson was pushing Tom and Nellie right along. As teamster he considered it his proper right to drive the gray team and resented every time Lincoln John chose to work with them himself. But he had no choice. He had to do things the way Lincoln John told him, just as Lincoln John had to accept Mr. Dunston's orders. It seemed to Natty that no matter where a person stood, there was always somebody else on top. He could feel sorry for Benson, though at the same time he was glad that he and Mr. John would have Kit and Charlie to themselves. Making the trip home with Benson would not seem the same thing at all.

Taking Framm's engine across the river bridge was to Natty a precarious procedure. A signboard at each end said "UNSAFE FOR LOADS OVER 10 TONS." But most people thought it would not safely carry that much. Nor did Framm know exactly how much his steam engine weighed. The only way to avoid it was to detour downriver three miles to the heavier bridge at Hawkinsville with another three miles up the other side, and nobody wanted to do this. So every year, Mr. John and the Framms took a deep breath, brisked up the horses, and started over. The drop to the river, twenty feet below, would have made a splash to remember. Lincoln John had told Natty to keep off until the engine was all the way across, so he stayed listening to the ominous thunder of the iron wheels upon the planks until the tires hit the gravel on the far side.

After that the only excitement was the steep pitch up onto the canal bridge, and here Kit and Charlie had to buckle into their collars. For a minute it seemed as if they were pulling Framm's horses as well as the engine, but they made the top without faltering, and the four horses with the engine, its smokestack rocking from side to side, went down the far side in a rush.

Lincoln John stopped them there for a breather and told Natty it would be best for him to stop here by the bridge while he and the Framms took the engine the rest of the way to Boyd's.

"Those two dogs they keep might likely act mean to a young pup like Bingo. I ain't going to be long."

So Natty waited while Bingo went fossicking along the canal bank for frogs. A few minutes later the jingle of loose trace links announced the return of Benson and the bay team. From where he sat in the grass, Natty watched them go up over the bridge and down the other side. After that the road stayed empty until Mr. John arrived with the gray team.

"Now," he said. "Here we be. We'll give you a hoist up onto Kit and see how you set. If it's good, I'll get onto Charlie. But if it ain't, we'll walk and nobody will know the difference."

To his surprise Natty found that sitting astride the big gray mare was nowhere near as painful as he had thought it might be. Her withers and backbone had none of the prominence of Charlie's, which made Natty realize why Mr. John suggested he ride Kit.

"It doesn't feel bad," he said, looking down into Lincoln John's mild eyes. "It doesn't hurt."

Mr. John smiled. "Then I'll just climb up onto this Charlie horse," he said, "and we can get to going."

The gray team walked with an unhurried stride that covered the ground in what had always seemed to Natty an amazing way; sitting on Kit's back, he was now equally amazed by the smoothness of her gait. The warmth of her rounded body under his thighs passed up into his. He found that

[*117*]

by taking hold of the brass knobs on the hames, he could keep himself tilted forward so that his bottom felt no pain at all. Every now and then Kit would turn her head and look at him from a back-slanted eye that was full, he thought, of amusement and pleasure too to see him where he was, and with Bingo running elatedly alongside, tongue flapping from the corner of his mouth and his head turned up in some sort of astonishment, Natty was swept suddenly by a happiness he had not felt in weeks.

As they rode towards home, Mr. John celebrated, if not Natty's unleashed happiness, a satisfaction of his own. "We have sure been lucky," he said, "getting through the whole of threshing without a rainy day. Now the line storm can come anytime she wants and I won't care a mite. No, not any mite at all."

"Is that the equinox?" asked Natty, who had recently heard his father use the word.

"It is," said Lincoln John. "Comes September twenty-third, or thereabouts, when the sun steps back over the equator." And for a moment Natty had an image, which he knew to be silly, of the sun playing hopscotch.

"Will it rain very hard?" he asked.

"Generally does," Mr. John replied. "Rains heavy, sometimes for a couple of days, sometimes for a week, sometimes even more than that. Then

the brook comes up, I can tell *you*. I have to open
the valve under the dam so the pond won't rise
over it." His tone suggested an element of peril in
which there was something to be relished. "But
that's a week away," he added. "Nothing to think
of now, with the threshing done. We can close up
the mow doors with the straw all in and dry."

The sun was still warm. Natty heard Bingo
barking in a muffled way. In a moment he saw the
pup with his head down a woodchuck hole and
then heard the answering, angry, whistled taunts
of the woodchuck himself.

"The marment's got his dander up," Mr. John
observed.

Bingo lost interest and came racing after the
horses as they turned out above the river to cross
the bridge, their hoofs, without the dampening roll
of the wheels behind them, making a splendid
thunder on the planks. Then, as they moved into
the comparative silence of the road beyond, a gun-
shot echoed across the meadows.

"That's your pa's Belgian gun," Mr. John said,
and Natty recognized it, too.

"He's up above the pond," Mr. John continued.
"He'd better get some shooting in before the line
storms start."

"Can't he hunt then?" Natty asked.

"It'll get too wet to suit him. When it's rained
three days or a week, the ground gets like a sponge

under your feet. Even if it ain't raining just then, a man gets soaked from the tree drips. And when it comes to that, the birds don't like moving either. If the rain stops for a while, though, after two or three days, some of them will come out of their hide-holes, but they are slow moving, slow flying." Mr. John turned his head to look at Natty. "If I was a boy like you, now, and if I wanted to go bird shooting, I'd go when the rain stops awhile, and I'd just creep along the path like a partridge myself, making no noise, and using my eyes to see everything all around me every two or three steps I took."

Natty suddenly could see himself creeping along a path as Mr. John described it. He didn't know if it was something he wanted to do. But he said, "George told me I could borrow his shotgun."

"Would your pa allow you to go out with a shotgun, Natty?"

"I don't know."

"You could ask him," said Lincoln John. "It wouldn't be good taking a shotgun out without he told you you could."

They had left the river road behind and were crossing the meadows, and Kit and Charlie had their ears pricked for the barn.

"Yes," Mr. John said thoughtfully. "A young

fellow like you, walking quiet all the time, might pretty likely find a bird in a break in the rain."

It was a new thought for Natty, and when his father returned late in the afternoon with Major, but without a bird, the idea came to him that if he himself could bring home a partridge it might make his father think a little better of him. He hardly listened to Mr. Dunston's account after supper of a long and unrewarding hunt clear to their back line.

"Put it down in the record as an abominable day, Natty. Abominably dry in the woods and Major abominably skittish and wild. I had three shots, but no real chances of dropping the bird."

"We heard you shoot when we were coming home," Natty volunteered.

"I was up at the head of the pond. Major flushed a bird on the other side of the brook. I had only a flashing glimpse and was lucky to get off a shot at all. I'm surprised you heard it, though."

"Mr. John said it sounded like your gun. He also said Bingo had the makings of a real cowdog," Natty went on. "Couldn't we keep him for a cow-dog on the farm?"

Natty realized that his father did not like the idea of what he considered a mongrel working on his place, but he tried once more.

"Redskin always got the Hollinses' cows all by

himself," he pointed out. "Mr. Hollins and Herschel didn't ever have to go to fetch them."

"They only have half a dozen head or so," Mr. Dunston said scornfully. "Those undersized Swiss animals. It isn't like rounding up our big herd of real Holsteins and bringing them back three-quarters of a mile to the barn. You might as well expect a drab little dog like that to fly!" His voice rankled with sarcasm and distaste. "Keeping a dog like Bingo on this place just doesn't make sense."

Natty tried to swallow the words that welled up in his throat, but his father must have heard some of them.

"What's that you said?" he asked ominously. "Say it so I can hear it."

Now Natty had to struggle to bring out the words he had wanted to say.

"I said Bingo's my dog. Mother gave him to me."

Mr. Dunston stared at his son in silence, as if he could not have heard correctly. When he did speak, his voice was controlled and cold.

"You've been, perhaps, too young to realize it, but you are old enough now to understand that everything in this place, and the house in New York for that matter, exists from the money *I* make with my work. That means most of this house, which I have added to the little house that was originally here. It means the farmhouse and the teamster's cottage that Lincoln John and Benson live in, and all the other buildings, and the animals and poultry. It even means you three children, because I pay for your clothes and your food and your schools and the doctor bills."

He broke off his recital momentarily, and Natty said in a tight, high voice, "But Mother gave him to me. She paid for him. I saw her do it. With her own money."

His father said, "I don't doubt she took the money out of her purse, but it was hers only in a sense." He paused to clear his throat. "It was hers because I had given it to her — though not, I may say, to buy a dog for you. This may be hard for you to understand, but it's time you began to get things clear, the way things really are in this life. Your mother's father was a minister and had no money to leave his children. Whatever your mother has comes entirely from me."

Staring up at his father, Natty had a bleak sensation of his words dissolving. He no longer saw his father's face; it had been replaced by that of his mother crying.

She had been sitting in the sunny window of her bedroom, in the small, low chair she used when she sewed; and as he went down the short passage, Natty's eyes were filled with the loveliness of her head — bent slightly forward, with the coil of dark hair on top, revealing the gentle line of her neck — and his breath caught as it always did when he saw her. In his eyes she was the most beautiful being on earth. But he noticed that instead of sewing she was holding a letter in her lap, and when she lifted her face at the sound of his approach, he saw the shining tear-tracks on her cheeks, and his heart turned over.

"Mummy!" he cried. "What is it?"

His voice, however, came out as little more than a whisper and her answer was equally soft.

"It's from Aunty Mamie," she said. "Aunt Nelly has been taken very ill and Aunty Mamie herself is not well and they need money. Quite desperately. Aunty Mamie doesn't know what to do."

The two aunts were tiny maiden ladies who lived together in a house, in Gloucester, almost as tiny as themselves, and they were favorites, especially Aunty Mamie, of the Dunston family. It was hard for Natty to see what so saddened his mother about their plight.

"Won't Daddy give you the money for them? If you ask him?"

"Oh yes," she said, but to his dismay he saw her tears coming back. "He's always generous about Aunty Mamie. But that's just it. I don't *want* to ask him. Oh, I wish I had *some* money of my own.

Only a little, but my own. So I could give money to Aunty without having to ask anybody. Not even Daddy."

He still did not quite see why she was crying and, sensing his perplexity, she tried to explain.

"It's just that I wish I could feel that I belonged to myself."

Even then he had not been able to truly understand why she was so upset; but now, listening to what his father said, he began to comprehend a little of what had troubled her, and in spite of the long interval, some of her sorrow and fear, amounting nearly to panic, invaded him. He stared at his father, seeing his face come clear again, with a kind of horror.

"I see," he said, and then, after a moment's hesitation, "I think I'll go to bed."

And as always his father had to light Natty's candle.

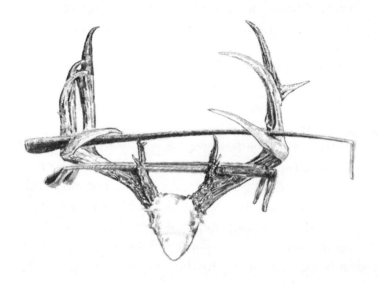

EIGHT

🌿 UPSTAIRS, he performed his usual routine for securing himself against the night, but he did not fall asleep for a long time. The image of his mother haunted him, seeming to confront his father, then fading to inevitable submission in which he himself shared; yet he felt that she was not on his side, any more than he himself could be of any help to her, for in his father's eyes he felt himself to be utterly of no account. After a while these thoughts began to blur and for a moment he thought of the ride home on the gray team with Mr. John, of what

Mr. John had told him about hunting partridges in a break in the equinoctial storm, and the idea of possibly shooting one himself to take back to the house recurred to him with increased vividness. As he at last drifted off to sleep, there was a soft sound of rain starting to fall on the roof outside his window.

It was still raining in the morning, but he felt certain it was not the line storm Mr. John had talked about; and as the day wore on, the sun broke through, slanting down bleak rays between the clouds. Mr. Dunston went off with Major an hour after lunch and several times Natty heard the reports of his shotgun. Though he came back with only one bird, he seemed unusually pleased, because it was a woodcock — a much more difficult bird to wing, he told Natty, than a partridge. Major had put it up in an alder tangle in the night pasture and fortunately Mr. Dunston's instantaneous reaction had been on the mark. He made no mention of the other shots Natty had heard.

So one day followed another. The shooting remained poor and on Natty's desk the record book remained blank.

Six nights later, the rain came back in force. Natty woke before daybreak to the roar of it on the roof and, above it, the tearing sound of wind in the pine trees around the house. When he got out of bed, the brook was coming up, and by noon it was nearly bank-high. Lincoln John came over after lunch to consult with Mr. Dunston about opening the valve beneath the dam.

"You think this rain's going to keep on?" Mr. Dunston asked.

"Line storm's nearly always big," Lincoln John replied. "Better open the valve too early than too late."

"Open it halfway," Mr. Dunston suggested. "If the pond keeps coming up you can open it more tomorrow."

Natty fetched Bingo from the barn and went up to the dam with Mr. John. Their stiff black rubber raincoats were identical, even to the fasteners — like the fasteners on galoshes. Of course, Natty's was only a small fraction of the size of Mr. John's. Still, in his eyes, they were look-alikes, and this gave him a sense of playing an important part in the proceeding. Mr. John carried what he called his "penstalk" on his shoulder. It was like a cross-handle socket wrench, but with two differences: instead of being an ordinary length, the stem was over six feet long, and instead of a socket at the end, there were two prongs to fit between the handle spokes of the sluice valve that was at the bottom of the vertical flue of plank. It took some fiddling to fit the prongs into the handle, but Mr. John was patient and unhurried.

"I've got her," he said after three or four minutes.

"Get down to the bottom if you want to see the water come out. But take care you don't slip in. She's going to make a boiling flood."

All summer the pool at the mouth of the sluice stood half-empty; what water it held was motionless and an evil rusty color. Natty hunkered down near the edge, the drip from the brim of his rubber rainhat onto his shoulders heavy enough to be felt. Bingo looked wetter than a muskrat but didn't seem to mind. He had his eyes, as Natty had his own, on the mouth of the two-foot tile that showed only an inch or two above the rusty pool. A third of the way up the dam, Mr. John began to turn his penstalk. It seemed to take a lot of effort to get started.

"There'll be a power of bottom mud packed in there," he explained. "It don't want the gate to lift, I guess."

He smiled slightly, looking down at the boy and his rain-soaked pup.

"She'll come easier the more she opens."

At the fourth turn of the penstalk a rumbling sound came from the tile and was repeated, as if deep inside somewhere the dam was experiencing indigestion. If Bingo's hair could have stood up it would have done so. Instead he growled. At the same instant a prodigious bubble heaved up through the rusty pool; it was dark brown and thick and erupted with a gaseous stench of rotted vegetation. Bingo leaped back and barked hysterically. Natty was too surprised to move. Gurgle followed gurgle, each one louder than the last. Suddenly the water in the pool was no longer rusty but the same dark, forbidding brown — worse, Natty thought, than black bean soup, which he never liked. Now the gurgling had turned into an interrupted roar and a flood of water rushed down the previously dry channel that led to the proper course of the brook.

Still Mr. John kept turning the penstalk, smiling when his eye met Natty's.

"Sixteen full turns opens her halfway," he said. "That means thirty-two of these half-turns, and I'm just twenty-six."

The mouth of the big tile had long since disappeared; a turgid burst of water overflowed the channel to join the brook. When Mr. John finished the last six half-turns of his penstalk and they started back across the dam and home to the farm, Natty wanted to race ahead to stand on the bridge by the house and see the crest of the flood come to him. But it was already too late. The brook had far outpaced him. By the time he stepped out on the bridge, it was hurtling down the slide beyond in uncontrolled turbulence; he stood watching it boil past the house foundation below until he found himself getting dizzy.

Mrs. Hollins looked at him and Bingo with bleak disapproval. "You'd better give him some supper and take a towel out to the barn and dry him off some. And then you better come straight back and take a hot bath yourself. Seems to me as if you'd done about everything a boy could think of to catch himself a cold."

He did not catch one, of course. With his raincoat, boots, and rubber hat, he had kept perfectly dry, as he could have pointed out to her. But he thought it better not to do so and duly followed her advice and joined his father at the supper table, still filled with excitement at the opening of the sluice. Rather to his own astonishment, he found himself telling about it. When he had described the huge bubble coming up, the exhalation of foul air, and Bingo's outraged reaction to it, he looked up to see his father smile. For a wild, exhilarating instant he imagined he had said something that had pleased his father. It was not so.

"Yes," Mr. Dunston said. "It's quite a sight. I'm not surprised it should scare a timid pair like you and that Bingo of yours."

He saw at once that his first assumption of his

father's smile as a shared amusement was false; Mr. Dunston was not smiling with but at him, and in coupling him with Bingo, he realized, his father had put him down another notch. He wanted to come to Bingo's defense, to point out that his reaction had sprung from outrage, not panic, but from his father's expression he knew it would be useless to try. He felt submerged in helplessness and when his father continued with mocking questions found it impossible to answer, sitting in glum silence until the meal was over. Soon after they adjourned to the living room, Mr. Dunston, perhaps weary of his own monologue, suggested that since Natty appeared to have nothing at all to say, he might as well take himself to bed.

Natty was relieved to go. As he climbed the stairs and started down the hall, he became aware once more of the storm. His bedroom seemed in the very heart of it. The downpour of rain on the roof outside his window, the rush of wind through the pines around the house, the roar of the brook, full-throated but at moments almost choked by its own flooding, battered the walls. After he blew out his candle, he lay listening in the absolute darkness and wondered whether the pond had risen higher against the dam.

It was still raining next morning. Above the bridge, floodwater reached a hundred feet into the meadow; it flowed between the icehouse and the carriage barn, making an island of the smaller building, and crossed the driveway in a shallow stream on the far side of the bridge. In his imagination the big house was now isolated from the life of the farm. Then, as he still watched the water moving in what was nearly an unbroken mass from the bridge to the back of the house, he saw a rig coming down the hill road above the pond and recognized it as the Hollinses' spring wagon, with Mr. and Mrs. Hollins on the seat, which surely meant the river had flooded the road.

Mrs. Hollins assured him of the fact when he came down to the kitchen. The road beyond their place also was under water. The only way to the Dunstons' was by driving across the sandflats above the valley and now the only way down to town would be over the bridge around by Boyd's. She doubted if Mr. Lewis would be coming with the mail for a few days. So did Natty after he had accoutered himself in boots and raincoat and gone out to the driveway bridge. To his astonishment, the brook was almost silent, and when he looked downstream he understood why. It no longer roared over rapids behind the house, for during the night the river had risen amazingly. It had not only flooded most of the river road, but had filled the lower meadows with lakes and come all the way up to the foundations of the house, so that the flood of the brook merged with river water far deeper than the rocks.

"I guess," said Mr. John, who had come over from the farm, "they've opened the sluices underneath the big dam above Forestport. Same as we've done here."

"Did you open the pond gate some more?" asked Natty.

"Yes," Mr. John replied. "Opened her as far as she could go this morning. I reckon this is the highest anybody's ever seen the river. Maybe ever will see. Norm Hollins said it's higher than he's ever heard tell of."

Together, in a kind of shared awe, they watched the downward rush of water without speaking. Then Lincoln John remarked that it was his opinion that the rain would stop in early afternoon, at least for a spell, if not for good — maybe an hour or two. It would be, he calculated, a good time for a boy to take a gun into the woods and look for a partridge — going slow and easy and using his eyes to look at everything there was before moving forward, as he had said before. It might be just the time for Natty if his pa was to give him the permission. Taking his dog with him, if he liked. The pup wouldn't make a difference, not being by nature a bird hunter.

"Do you think so, really?" Natty asked. And Lincoln John nodded. "Yes, I do."

Natty felt extremely hesitant about asking his father if he could take George's gun into the woods, but finally, at the end of luncheon, he worked up enough nerve.

"George said I could if I cleaned the barrel well afterwards," he added.

"George had no business telling you you could take it without asking me. You're only twelve, Natty. George didn't get the gun before he was thirteen, and he was much bigger as well."

This was the kind of preamble to refusal that Natty had expected and he was resigning himself to disappointment when Mr. Dunston added, "But I don't know why not. Your notion of looking for birds in this weather is insane. Lord knows what you'll think of next. One thing, though, there'll be nobody else in the woods, so you won't be able to shoot someone. Unless you happen to hit that pup of yours. You'd be wise to leave him at home. What cartridges are you planning to use?"

Natty said that George had told him to take his. "So long as I paid for the ones I shot off."

"I see," Mr. Dunston said. "And how many will you be able to buy from George?"

"I've got money enough for three," Natty told him, turning red. His parents were continually pointing out how much money George earned compared to him. Because he was an industrious boy and didn't go wandering off doing nothing the way Natty did.

"Well, go along if you want to. The woods will be like the inside of a sponge. And stay well away from the river.'"

"I'm going to wear my raincoat," Natty said. "I'm going to go through the woods to the Hollinses', and then I'll come back across the flats."

NINE

❧ THE WOODS, when he entered them, were a different world from any he had known. The rain had stripped the trees of leaves, except for occasional beech trees. Under his boots the ground felt soft; when he walked across a bed of moss the water squished up around his feet, covering his insteps. He could hear the sound it made as he kept walking, as slow as he was able, and trying to see everything there was on the ground around him. He could only see a little way off the trail because the dampness made a mist between the trees. The air felt heavy as he breathed and it was loaded with the scent of balsam, though the trees themselves were still some hundred feet ahead. It seemed a long time before, in his slow progress, he finally entered their shadowy world.

Here there was less underbrush, but in the fringes of the stands of balsam and spruce, young trees were densely packed so that he had the feeling of walking between walls or, as he thought of them, palisades. Somewhere to his right and a long way off, he heard Bingo giving excited barks.

The young dog had been almost delirious with excitement and joy at being released from the barn on what he had surely known to be an unlikely day for any sort of expedition. He had been briefly fascinated by the shotgun Natty was carrying but had lost interest in it almost at once. As soon as they entered the woods, Bingo had rushed off on his own. It was perhaps just as well. Stiff and awkward inside his black rubber coat, Natty had two or three times tried bringing the shotgun to his shoulder, aiming at a moss-covered nubbin or at any other object his imagination could conjure into game. His effort to bring up the barrel into firing position was made still more difficult by the canvass pouch he wore slung by a strap over his shoulder, for he owned nothing like his father's shooting jacket with its game pocket. As Bingo's barks faded out, he tried aiming the gun once more. Then he went forward two steps and halted to look, first to

one side, then to the other, and ahead, the way
Lincoln John had suggested.

He was astonished by the things he began to see.
The tip of a chipmunk's nose in a tiny hole between the forked roots of a spruce tree. In a moment he caught the shine of its eye farther back
and knew he in turn was being watched. Just before the next bend of trail, he glanced up. Ten or
twelve feet over his head two screech owls, side by
side, clung to a balsam branch; they were motionless; an earlier time his eye would have passed over
their huddled forms without seeing them for birds.
It was as though a new force drew his eyes to what
was to be seen. Also, he seemed able to look farther
between the close-standing trunks of trees. It was
perhaps why he knew, as he moved around the
bend, that a partridge was standing in the trail, and
he began to bring the shotgun to his shoulder.

There were two birds, one walking close behind
the other. They were very erect, their heads as
high as their necks would stretch. They must, he
thought, be listening for Bingo's barks, which
he could no longer hear but they perhaps could.
Whatever it was that kept their attention en-
thralled, they were wholly unaware of Natty's
presence behind them. As he finished raising the
gun to aim, his raincoat made a creaking sound and
instantaneously they took flight. His heart pound-
ing, he pulled the trigger, certain that he was too

slow. In the damp, heavy air the report was deafening, and the kick of the gun was much heavier than he had expected. For a moment he stood dazed, with closed eyes. When he opened them, he saw both birds lying on the trail.

It was hard to believe what he had done. He broke the shotgun and pulled the expended shell from the breech and put it in a pocket of his trousers. Then he went forward and crouched to look at the two birds. They were quite dead. The wave of elation that had been mounting in him was tinged with sadness as he studied the beautiful markings of their feathers, the black ruffs one of them wore. But the sadness faded quickly. He saw that he had done something remarkable, even if it had been pure chance. He had never heard of anyone killing two birds with one shot. Then he realized that no one, least of all his father, would believe that he had done so, and after a minute he stood up, loaded the gun with a second shell, and fired it into the sky. If anyone had heard him shoot, they would have heard two shots — to account for his two birds.

If the first shot had not registered on Bingo, the second had, for he arrived full-pelt, his tongue flapping out a mile. The birds on the trail interested him, but only mildly. After nudging them with his nose, he bounced over to Natty. The irrational hope Natty had once indulged in — that

Bingo might become a real dog for finding partridges or woodcock and so win Mr. Dunston's approval — evaporated for good.

He bent over to pick up the birds, one after the
other, and put them into his canvass pouch. When
he slung it behind his back again, the two bodies made a comfortable weight. Then he broke
the shotgun again and took out the second spent
shell. He started to put it in his pocket with the
first but decided not to. There would be no way
of telling which had brought down the two partridges. He put the second shell in his raincoat
pocket. The first shell he would put on his bureau, where he could see it from his bed whenever
he wanted.

To all these moves, Bingo had paid close,
if slightly puzzled, attention; but now, as Natty
started off along the trail at a normal pace, he exploded with pleasure, racing forward, then back
again, first on one side, then on the other, plainly
intending to give Natty close escort for the rest of
their walk.

They went now at a normal pace, for Natty was
no longer interested in finding partridges or any
other game. He had never seen the woods so wet.
Where springs normally crossed the trail, the
water was no longer running but still, forming a
shallow pond. The rise in the river had forced the
water back and must in fact be moving through the

road culverts in the wrong direction. His intention of returning across the flats had been more sensible than he realized, for the river road was under water. Where it ran across the beaver meadows it would obviously be neck-deep in flood. And a little short of the Hollinses' place, water had reached so far inland that he and Bingo were obliged to leave the trail they had been following for one on higher ground. From it he could look down through the nearly leafless trees to the road. But it was gone. The water stretched unbroken across it and through the trees, to the slope he and Bingo walked along. The road reappeared only when it too climbed the slope on the Hollinses' land. Joining it, Natty and Bingo came out at the Hollinses' barn-yard.

Mr. Hollins and Herschel were hitching their team to the lumber wagon. As he came close to the wagon, Bingo lifted his muzzle. His tail drooped and stiffened and he began to whine.

"What's the matter with you?" Natty demanded.

"He can tell," Herschel said. "Redskin's dead. We've got him in the wagon and we're taking him up on the flat to bury him. By the sugar shanty. He always liked it there."

Natty put one foot on a wheel hub and pulled himself up to look into the wagon box. Redskin lay there, stretched on his side, his eyes closed, his lips slightly drawn to show a little of his old, brownish teeth, one canine broken off at the tip. He looked dead, but not the way animals looked on a farm when they had been slaughtered. There was a lot of death on a farm, especially as large a one as Mr. Dunston owned and ran, because the animals had to be used for food. Sometimes Natty thought there was as much death as life on the farm. But it was different with Redskin.

"He died in his sleep," Mr. Hollins said, as if that explained it. "During the night, I calculate. He was an old dog. But he was a good one. He worked right up to the end of his life."

There didn't seem to be anything else to say. After a moment Mr. Hollins cleared his throat and turned to Natty.

"Why don't you ride up with us? Then you can walk back across the flats."

"Thank you," Natty said. "It won't be such wet going."

"That was the idea." Mr. Hollins took hold of the reins and climbed up to the wagon seat. "You get up here with me," he told Natty. "Herschel can ride in back, with Redskin. That gun of yours loaded?"

"No," Natty replied. He broke the gun to show the empty chamber. Mr. Hollins exclaimed,

"Pshaw! You didn't need to do that. You tell me your gun is empty. I believe you."

Natty felt the blood rushing into his face, pleased that Mr. Hollins considered his word good as a man's. He handed the gun up to Mr. Hollins, who gave it back as soon as Natty was seated, and clucked at the horses.

As they followed the road slanting up to the flats, Natty saw that Bingo, instead of running alongside or in front of the team, as he usually did at home, was trotting just behind the rear wheels, and he wondered if this was because of the dead Redskin. Mr. Hollins had also taken notice and approved it.

"That's a smart little dog you've got," he observed. "He'd make an easy learner, I believe."

To his own surprise, Natty found himself emboldened to broach an idea that had begun to take shape in his mind while he watched Bingo indifferently poking the dead partridges with his nose.

"Do you think," he asked hesitantly, "that Bingo could maybe take Redskin's place?"

Mr. Hollins was silent so long that Natty began to think he had been offended by the question. But he hadn't. He answered with a question of his own.

"How do you mean that?"

"Well, if he lived here with you and learned to get the cows with Herschel, could he learn after a while to get them by himself, like Redskin?"

"I think probably he could," Mr. Hollins said. "But I wouldn't want him here, just boarding for the winter. You teach a dog to do what he ought, you don't want to see him go away in half a year."

"Oh no," Natty said. "I meant, if I gave him to you and Herschel, to keep here. For him to belong to you. My father doesn't like him. To see him around our place." He paused. "Bingo'd like living with you, I think."

"Well," Mr. Hollins said. "If that's what you mean, we'll take him. If he don't learn to earn his keep, we'll find him some place to live, unless you wanted him back."

"I'd rather see him living over here with you," Natty said.

"When do you plan to bring him over?"

"I'd like to keep him until we go back to New York," Natty said. "If that's all right for you."

"It is," Mr. Hollins said. Herschel had said not a word, but when Natty looked back towards him he seemed pleased.

A moment later Mr. Hollins stopped the team, where the back road led across the flats and down to the Dunstons' buildings. Natty climbed down over the wheel.

"We heard you shoot two times," Mr. Hollins said. "Did you have any luck?"

"Two partridges," Natty told him, and as he watched the Hollinses' rig move on along the road, he realized with astonishment that he had not even thought of the birds all the time he had been with Mr. Hollins and Herschel.

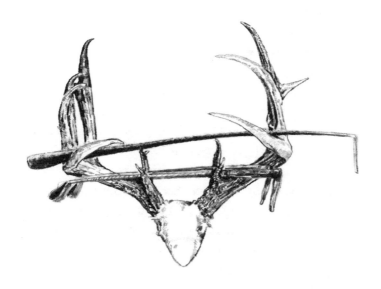

TEN

❧ IT WAS close to dark when Natty came through
the kitchen door, leaving Bingo outside on the
porch to wait for his supper. Mrs. Hollins was
stirring next morning's oatmeal and she put the
double saucepan at the back of the stove before she
turned around to watch him unsling his canvass
pouch and plop it onto the kitchen table.

"You got something, Natty!" she exclaimed.

Instead of answering he drew first one bird, then
the other from the pouch and arrayed them side by
side.

"My!" she said. "Those are nice birds. They

look bigger than them your pa has shot so far."
She felt them with her small, confident fingers.
"They're real well fleshed. My! You're a better
shot than you've been allowed to be, Natty."

She made him feel proud, but he said, "I was
lucky," which he knew to be the fact even if she
didn't, and went to clean George's gun before putting it back in its place, leaving Mrs. Hollins to
make string nooses to hang his birds by.

As soon as he entered the toolroom, where the
gun oil and cleaning rods were kept, the door to the
living room opened and his father, standing against
the lamplight, looked in.

"You were gone a long time," he said. "I wondered what had become of you, after I heard those
two shots. Were they your shots?"

"Yes," Natty told him. "I stopped by the Hollinses' for a while and they gave me a ride up onto
the flats as far as the back road. They were taking
Redskin up in the wagon to bury him by their
sugar shanty. Redskin was dead."

Mr. Dunston said in a dry voice, "I gathered he
must be dead if they were going to bury him. I'm
sorry but he wasn't really much of a dog."

By "much of a dog" Mr. Dunston actually
meant he was not well bred, as Natty well understood, but at that moment he felt resentful and
angry. "Redskin got their cows for them as good as
any man could," he said.

Mr. Dunston disregarded Natty's tone but corrected his grammar. "He didn't fetch them as *good*. He fetched them as *well* as any man could. I'm sorry for the Hollinses. They'll miss him."

"Yes, they will," Natty said.

"Bring me your candle to light when you're done in here. You'll need it for changing for supper."

"I'll bring it," Natty said, "when I've fed Bingo his supper and hung my partridges in the ice-house."

"Partridges!" Mr. Dunston had turned into the living room but now he spun back. "Do you mean to say *you* shot a *partridge?* This isn't your idea of a joke, is it?"

"No. It isn't. I got a partridge. I got two of them."

"With two shots? You fired those two shots?"

"Yes. I fired them."

"I don't believe it."

Mr. Dunston went out of the living room and Natty heard him hurrying towards the kitchen. He didn't know quite how it made him feel to have those two birds on the kitchen table to confound his father. But he did know he could never get the inside of George's shotgun as bright as the barrels of either of his father's guns. George, it appeared, had not been much concerned about the condition of his own gun. After a minute Natty gave up on the job, took the gun to the rack in the dining room, and then went into the kitchen. His father was still examining the two birds as if he was trying to convince himself that they were real. Mrs. Hollins, who had been watching him with an expressionless face, looked up at Natty's entrance.

"I've fed Bingo," she told him. "You'd better put him to bed and take your partridges with you when you go. That is, if your pa is done looking them over."

"Yes. Yes." Mr. Dunston turned with a start and looked at his son. Natty could not fathom what was behind the blue stare of his father's eyes. He took up the birds wordlessly and joined Bingo outside on the porch.

As they crossed the bridge over the hissing floodwater of the brook, Natty saw Mr. John come out of the farmhouse and walk slowly towards him through the bars of light slanting from the windows.

"So you had some luck," he said. "I seen you come back and go up on your kitchen porch, but I couldn't tell if you'd got anything."

"I did," Natty said, holding them up. Lincoln John slipped his fingers through the loops to heft the partridges.

"My, that's fine, Natty."

"It was just the way you said it might be," Natty said. "If I hadn't been going the way you said to go, I wouldn't have come up so close on them. One was ahead of the other. I put the gun up and fired it, I think just as they began to fly. I think they must have flown into my shot, Mr. John."

"You got them with one shot. My, my. That was surely something. And then you had a shot at another bird?"

"No," Natty told him. "I didn't think my father would believe me. So I fired that other shot just up into the air."

"Well," Mr. John said. "It's hard to know what any man is going to believe. Or not believe. But I figure it happened just how you said."

Natty glowed with pleasure to hear him say that; and he felt even better when Mr. John not only went into the icehouse with him to hang the partridges from hooks in the meat room but walked with him as far as the barn, claiming that he wanted to be sure the men had closed the sliding doors; and then, after Bingo had been put to bed, he went back with Natty as far as the bridge, where he said good night, adding, "You've had yourself quite a day, Natty."

His words gave Natty's feelings another boost, which continued all the way up to his room. Before starting to bathe and change, he sat down at his desk and opened the game record, finding the right page by the heading dates he had written in. Under September 25 he put down his shooting the two birds pretty much in the words he had used to tell Mr. John about it. When he had finished he read the entry through, experiencing the same mixture of surprise, pleasure, and wonder he had felt in the rain-drenched woods. But then, as he began to turn the pages he had left blank over the past weeks, a sense of guilt began to grow. In some strange way it seemed unfair to have written about himself and left his father's partridges without mention. He could see the enormity of his behavior and he tried to remember on which days his father had come home with game.

He discovered that he could remember nothing. As he stared at the empty pages, he realized that he would never be able to recall a single item of the reports his father had given of an afternoon's hunting. What was worse, in omitting to make the required entries, he had not only been directly disobedient; in his assurances that he had made them, he had lied to his father a dozen times. He knew what the consequences would be: Mr. Dunston had spelled them out in formidable detail.

When, after his bath, he started putting on clean clothes, he found his hands clumsy. It was a struggle to get his shirt and trousers buttoned — not because his hands were cold, which they were, but because he had become afraid. In some manner unclear to him, his shooting of the two partridges had brought much closer the time when

Mr. Dunston would demand to see the game record. Suddenly he saw again his father's flushed, furious face and his hand reaching for the African quirt on the deer horns.

He tried to conjure up expedients, but none would come into his muddled mind. He thought of calling down the back stairs to ask Mrs. Hollins to tell his father he felt too sick to come to supper. But even if his father did not come up to see him, she would certainly do so and would quickly see that he was not ill but only terrified and he could not possibly tell her why. And worse, if his father did come up, he might — he probably would — ask to have a look at the game record. In the end he forced himself to leave his room. He was only just in time, for as he entered the dining room, Mr. Dunston was in the act of seating himself.

"You're late, Natty. However," he added with a slight smile, "in the case of a gunner of such prowess, I suppose we should make an allowance."

Natty felt himself flush. Though grateful at not being taken to task for his lateness — Mr. Dunston was rigidly insistent on punctuality, at least for others — he was uncertain of what his father actually meant. When, after Mrs. Hollins had brought in the first course, he mustered the courage to look up, his father's eyes met his in a cold speculative stare.

"Those shots you fired were pretty close together," he remarked. Not knowing what he was expected to say, Natty said nothing. His father continued: "So the birds must have been close together, too. Weren't they?"

"Yes," Natty said. "They were."

"Most boys would have been too excited picking up the first bird to be able to make the second shot." Mr. Dunston put a forkful of Mrs. Hollins's goulash in his mouth and with electrifying suddenness turned his eyes on his son. "What do you think, Natty?"

Again, not knowing what to say, Natty mumbled that he didn't know.

"It's my opinion that you were just lucky," Mr. Dunston said. "I'll be interested to read what you put in the game record about it. We can compare your experience with some of mine. Two sportsmen comparing shots," Mr. Dunston added in a jocular tone. He raised his napkin to his lips, wiping the underside of his mustache in the fastidious manner that had always looked faintly ridiculous to Natty but that now, for some reason he did not understand, was intimidating. He found himself holding his breath as his father went on. "I sent Jody around to Boyd's to get the mail from town this afternoon and he brought a letter from Mother. Bessie, for once, appears to be well, but I'm afraid Mother is not. She's seen Dr. Chisolm and he wants her in a hospital for a going-over. He's made a date for the fifth of October. Therefore we'll go down on the fourth — a week from Monday. We'll have Sunday evening here and can go over the game record after supper."

ELEVEN

❧ AT LAST he was in his bedroom again, the door bolted behind him. It had seemed that the evening would never end or that — most horribly worse — his father would have a sudden inclination to look over the game record then and there. But he had occupied himself writing Natty's mother about the plans for their return, while Natty pretended to read. Perhaps Mr. Dunston also felt tension, for, after he had finished the letter, he said, "You must feel tired after your exciting afternoon."

"Yes. A little," Natty answered, and accepted

his father's suggestion that since it was near bedtime anyway he might like to go up at once. He
had tried not to show his relief, going through the
customary motions of fetching his candle for Mr.
Dunston to light, saying the usual good-night in
what seemed a fairly normal voice, and walking
out into the hall. But by the time he reached the
stairs, he was trembling.

Even when he was safe in his room, he was unable to control his shaking, and after a minute he
put the candle on his desk and sat down with the
game record in front of him, staring at it as if in
some miraculous way the notes he had never written down might materialize in his own hand-
writing. He recalled hearing in church that if a
person had complete faith he could accomplish
anything, but after a time he found that he had in-
sufficient faith. The pages remained blank and his
trembling uncontrollable.

On a sudden impulse he blew out his candle.
Darkness did not help, so he got up and felt his
way to the bureau, pulled out the drawer, and
found his box of matches. Back at the desk, he
struck one and relighted his candle with his own
match. His hands had stopped shaking and he sat
down again, finding his mind clearer, with a kind
of cold and speculative sense, as he began to search
for some solution to the predicament he had en-
meshed himself in.

From nowhere the idea occurred to him of just writing up the record out of his head. He knew how many partridge hung in the icehouse. He would just put down one or two birds for each successful day and for the unlucky ones he would write, "No luck," or "Very gusty winds. Major wild as a March hare," and phrases of that sort, which were favorites of his father's. They would, it seemed to him, lend conviction and possibly persuade Mr. Dunston that was what he had actually told his son, if Natty was determined enough to stick to his guns. "That's what you told me to write down," he would insist. And for a few splendid moments, he felt that as long as the total number of birds in the record checked out correctly, he could carry the thing off.

But then he knew he could not. Under those ice blue, accusing eyes his courage would collapse and the record would be exposed as a fraud, which would immeasurably intensify his father's anger. There was no way out. Only seven days remained until that Sunday. He saw himself moving from one day to another, the way a condemned man in the prison deathhouse moved from one cell to the next as each prisoner ahead of him left it empty in his progress to the electric chair.

He had read about that in their New York paper the winter before. His mother told his father in a low voice that the story should be kept from the children and so the paper was sent immediately downstairs to the kitchen. But Natty knew that anything sensational would not be thrown away until the maids had wrung every possible excitement from it. In the late afternoon, when the cook had run out on an errand, he had slipped downstairs and found the paper, sure enough, lying open to the story on the kitchen table. He had read every word of it. Like the doomed criminal, he himself had nothing left but to count the decreasing hours before his own destruction.

A guttering of the candle brought him back to the bedroom; the wick flared brightly in the puddle of melted wax. When he looked at his dollar watch it had stopped, and he realized that in his hurry to get down to supper before it was too late, he had forgotten to wind it. Only a few moments were left to him now to get undressed and into bed before the candle went out entirely. Afterwards, lying in darkness that was made alive by the hissing sound of the bank-high brook, he watched an image of himself stumbling towards the fatal door along the corridor of cells that the newpaper people called death row.

The voice of the brook was still in his ears when he woke, but the tone was different. Once more he could hear the roar of it at the end of the house, and he thought that the river water must have started to recede. As soon as he got out of bed, he knew that the weather had changed. It was colder. From his window he could see ghostly columns of mist rising beyond the dam. The sun was just up, and the sky at last was blue again, but with lines of pewter-colored clouds rolling down from the northwest. Then he saw the figure of Lincoln John near the foot of the dam. He was bending over his penstalk handle at the sluice gate valve. He must be shutting it down.

Later, after breakfast, Mr. John joined him on the bridge and reported Natty had been right. "Closed her down thirty half-turns. About half-way. The pond's gone down a good fraction, but it's too soon to shut the sluice the whole way." He looked over the rail of the bridge. "It won't show here for a while, but you'll see a difference by suppertime."

"Do you think the river's going down, too?" asked Natty.

"I haven't paid much mind to the river. It's the pond that had me worried. But yes," Mr. John said, squinting to look down the slide. "Yes, I do believe it has pulled back some from the house. You can hear the brook commencing to roar again. No doubt they're closing the gates under that dam at Forestport the way I closed down ours." His mild gaze turned back to Natty. "Any time you can hear the brook, you don't have to worry about the river being too high."

It was strange to think that stillness might harbor a more fearful threat of danger than tumult. In the big house things seemed to be the other way around. Whenever Mr. Dunston's raised voice echoed above the stairs or below, not only Natty but everyone else checked over their recent actions for things done wrong or left undone. At least today Natty, because it was Sunday, was not under obligation to take or get the mail; and in any case, the river was still too deep over the river road for Mr. Lewis and his old white horse to get through.

But to everybody's amazement, they came on Monday morning. They came over the river bridge and up the back road to the barn. In the yard Mr. Lewis sorted the mail for the place while Natty, with Bingo bounding excitedly alongside, ran to the house to collect the letters to go. When he returned, Mr. Lewis was in conversation with Lincoln John.

"They told me downriver that the water was over the road only in a couple of places below Hollinses'. So I figured to come in the back way and go up over the flats to the Hollinses'. After that Benjamin will wade us through the wet spots. He knows the road all right."

"He sure does," Lincoln John replied. "That old

animal could read a book if he didn't have to haul you and the mail."

"Wouldn't surprise me if he could," Mr. Lewis agreed. "But he didn't like turning off the road to come in this back way. That's why I had to stop reading and take hold of the reins."

The notion tickled Lincoln John's funny bone, and he was still smiling when Natty rejoined them with the letters to go. Mr. Lewis took them and gave him the letters he had brought. There seemed to be more than usual; on top he saw an envelope from his mother and under it another, also from her, both addressed to his father. This was unusual and suddenly chilled him with a premonition of disaster. He stood in silence while Mr. Lewis said good-bye and clicked his tongue for Benjamin. The old white horse started willingly enough; he often came up to the big house when on rainy days there was a package too big for the letter box. This was familiar ground to him; but when the mailman pulled on the reins to turn him towards the pond and the track over the flats, he dropped his head sulkily and let his ears droop. "Like a mule," Lincoln John remarked with a chuckle. "Mr. Lewis won't get any reading done, I bet. Not until Benjamin gets back on the river road."

He took the letters for his own house from Natty. There was nothing for Benson, but then there almost never was except when once a year the Sears, Roebuck catalogue came to everybody. The teamster and his wife lived very much to themselves.

He carried the mail into the living room and placed it on his father's desk. It was a relief when Mr. Dunston said, "Just leave them. I don't want to break off right now. I'll open the letters later."

Natty did not know what to do with himself. He wandered into the parlor and let his eyes rove blindly over the titles on the spines of the books. He had finished *Dr. Jekyll and Mr. Hyde,* but in the desultory drifting of his thoughts he might as well have never read it. When he went into the kitchen, it was empty. Then he saw Mrs. Hollins across the brook in conversation with Mrs. John. Bingo, on the kitchen porch, saw him at once and whapped his tail on the floorboards, but there wasn't time enough to do anything with Bingo before lunch. So he went up to his room to stare at the game record — but not to touch it — and emptied his mind of thoughts of any kind until he heard the slam of the kitchen door and shortly afterwards Mrs. Hollins calling up the back stairs that Mr. Dunston had already sat down at the table.

As soon as he entered the room, Natty knew from his father's face that something had gone wrong. He slipped into his seat as inconspicuously as possible and kept silent. Nothing was said as long as Mrs. Hollins was in the room, but the moment she left through the swinging door, Mr. Dunston burst out, "Your mother writes that she is going into the hospital earlier than planned. It seems Dr. Chisolm thinks it would be better so, and more convenient for him. Nobody, apparently, seems to have thought of consulting *me.*"

He took a mouthful of food from his plate, started to choke, and sipped from his water glass.

"We'll have to return tomorrow. I shall send Jody over with a note for the stationmaster to reserve two berths on the night train." The flush in his cheeks deepened. "This afternoon's the last one left me to go shooting and maybe add a bird or two to those we'll take down with us. It seems mighty little after all the days of rain we've had."

His eyes suddenly turned on Natty.

"Can you pack your trunk?"

"Yes," Natty said.

"I thought your mother packed you boys' trunks."

"She packs George's. I do my own."

"Well, then, I don't have to worry about that. I'm going to take Major up the south side of the pond to the back line. What do you intend to do?"

"I'll go for a walk with Bingo. Over to the Hollinses'." Natty waited a moment. "Is Mother very sick?" he asked his father.

"I don't expect so. She's always had frail health.

Probably this is just another of her spells of feeling poorly."

It didn't seem like a right answer to Natty. He didn't know how he could press his question, for he saw that his father was not in a mood to reply.

"Tonight," Mr. Dunston announced, "I want you to bring down the game record for me to see. After you've entered this afternoon's results."

He got up abruptly, leaving the dining room to go upstairs for his shooting clothes. Natty stayed frozen on his chair. Time had run out for him. This morning there had been seven days before he would have to confront his father, which seemed now a wonderfully long period, in which anything might happen to change the pattern of events. Now he had only one afternoon. Mrs. Hollins found him there, staring unseeingly towards the window, when she came in to clear the table.

"Is something the matter, Natty?" she asked.

"Yes," he said.

"Is there anything I can do?"

"No," he said, and then, "No, thank you."

He went out of the room, leaving her staring after him, and climbed the stairs to his bedroom. From his window he saw his father, shotgun cradled in his left arm, crossing the bridge toward the barn, to which Major had been moved at the beginning of the equinoctial storm (and hardly too soon, for his yard and kennel were now under water). A moment later the spaniel's delirious barking exploded the afternoon; his black body issued from the barn like a bullet, ears wildly flying, and hurtled for the woods, while Mr. Dunston hurried in his wake, blowing on his useless whistle.

The coast was clear. He went out to find Bingo. He was not waiting in his usual place on the kitchen porch; Mrs. Hollins said she had last seen him crossing the barnyard, and Natty found him in the barn. He was no longer in the box stall at the end of the cow run. Lincoln John had moved his barrel into an empty stall in the stable at the other end, because the stall in which he had been was where Major always spent the winter. "Your pa," he explained, "told me to move Bingo out and let Major have the place he's used to. But it's all right; it's warm in there with the horses."

Probably that was so, Natty thought, but the windows in the horse stable were all high up and small, and he resented his dog being put in such a place. But suddenly he realized that it was no darker than where Redskin had had his bed in the Hollinses' barn. He found that a comforting thought and, in a vague way he could not have defined, prophetic.

Bingo greeted him with pleasure and came willingly. They went up on the flats, taking their time, following the road along which he had returned when Mr. Hollins and Herschel had dropped him off on their way to bury Redskin. They walked slowly, one in each wheel track, through the rough grass. Bingo, with a dog's ability to divine Natty's trouble state, made none of his customary loops or forays but trudged abreast. The two figures of small boy, small dog seemed to creep across the extent of flatland like dull insects. Natty had said he was going to the Hollinses', but he now had no inclination to see anyone. Instead, when he reached their road along the boundary of the Dunston land, he turned towards the woods and the sugar shanty to which they had been taking Redskin for burial.

It was not difficult to find the grave. Bingo sensed its whereabouts at once, trotting around behind the shanty and making noises that were half whine, half yelp. A low pile of big cobblestones covered it. They were not for a marker, Natty realized, but to keep the old dog's body from being dug up. He sat on a nearby log and Bingo sat in front of him, both staring gloomily at the piled stones. Natty was aware of a great emptiness in himself. He thought that Redskin was lucky, lying there, with nothing more to worry about, and then it came to him that he himself would be better off if he were dead.

He could kill himself. He imagined himself going back for George's gun — he would still have time to go down and come back before dark, and he still had one cartridge left. He would sit on the stones over Redskin's grave and put the muzzle in his mouth — somewhere he had heard or read that that was how such things were done. But the barrel of George's shotgun was too long for him to reach the trigger with the muzzle in his mouth. The only way for him to pull it would be with his foot. He would have to take his shoe off and then his stocking and push the trigger with his great toe. In his mind's eye an image formed of his bare foot, cold and white in the damp air, the toe curled to grasp the trigger, and he was seized by a revulsion so intense he knew he could never kill himself like that even though it was the only possible way it could be done. He would have to go home and wait for what was going to happen.

TWELVE

❧ WHATEVER blue the sky had had was gone. A gray mist was moving down on the flatland as it sometimes did, leaving the river valley and the buildings of the farm still in clear air. It seemed another reason for him to start home. He had no idea how long he and Bingo had been sitting by Redskin's grave. But the dog was more than ready to move and started off from the shanty in a rush. When they came out of the sugar bush, the mist seemed to enclose the flatland in a kind of twilight. He might well have missed seeing Herschel walking the Hollinses' cows to their barn if Bingo had not suddenly given a low bark and squirmed under the wire fence.

The pup joined Herschel behind the little herd of ten, as if driving them home were a job he was accustomed to, and when Herschel came over to his side of the fence to walk abreast of Natty, Bingo kept to his position at the cows' heels.

"Acts just as if he knew what he was doing," Herschel remarked.

"Maybe he'll be a good cowdog," Natty said, uncertainly.

"Could be," Herschel agreed. "Of course, he's got to be learned where the cows hang out rainy days. And how to count to ten, or anyway how many cows we have, so's to get all of them. But I guess he'll do that pretty quick. My pa's good at telling animals things. Maybe in a year he'll know all by himself when it's time to go and fetch them." He grinned suddenly at Natty. "Just the same, until he does learn it, I'll like having him for company up here."

He didn't ask Natty when Mr. Dunston expected to be going back to the city. And Natty felt no inclination to let him know that it would be tomorrow night. They parted where the road across the Dunston land branched off. It took a bit of coaxing to get Bingo to abandon what he already seemed to consider his cows, but once the idea that he must leave them was established, the dog came willingly enough.

Boy and dog were halfway home when they heard two shots in the woods above the pond. Later, two more sounded. Natty took Bingo's supper out to him on the kitchen porch and sat down on the steps. About the time Bingo got to the stage of polishing his pan, with a good deal of clanging about on the floorboards, Natty saw his father coming down from the pond. Major was at his heels, plodding like a tired dog; but from the way Mr. Dunston strode along, Natty felt sure that he had had some luck. Mr. Dunston confirmed this almost at once.

"Three partridge," he announced, leading the way into the kitchen and fishing the birds one by one from his game pocket to lay them on the drainboard of the sink. "Nimrod himself could hardly have shot better."

Mrs. Hollins said admiringly, "Think of that!"

"You can take them out to the icehouse when you go to put your dog to bed, Natty. Take Major, too, and ask Lincoln John to give him his supper. Then come back to clean my gun and while you're doing it I'll tell you about my afternoon — for the game record."

It seemed to Natty as he cleaned the gun in the toolroom that his father's self-esteem did not weaken as he described his three successful shots, all difficult, the last a snap shot at a quartering bird against the last faint western light.

"Yes," he said, taking the gun from Natty and looking through the barrels, "you've done very well. Now go up and write the entry in the record book and get ready for supper. We'll look at it together afterwards."

He was in such obvious high spirits that Natty allowed himself to think his father might feel lenient when he saw the empty notebook. But almost instantly he knew that was not possible. His father's anger would boil over. The blank pages would not only infuriate him, he would see them as an insult. Out of nowhere came the realization that that was exactly what he had intended, knowing at the same time how it would fuel the ferocity of the whipping he would get, and now, in the terror of that knowledge, the muscles in his back and buttocks clenched with such rigidity that for a moment he was unable to move.

Even when his muscles began to relax, it was as much as he could do to pull his shirt off over his head. When he started to take down his drawers before getting into his bath, he found them stuck to his rump as they had been during the first days after his whipping. He had to soak them off as Mrs. Hollins had taught him.

He could not understand why this had happened. Perhaps the state of terror into which he was now stumbling had started the welts running again. He bathed and got dressed in a half-unconscious numbness and put off going downstairs until Mrs. Hollins called up that she was about to put supper on the table.

He took one last look at the notebook, wondering how he could have been fool enough not to have done what his father had wanted. Now it was too late. He took his candle from the desk and went downstairs.

Again, Mr. Dunston had already taken his chair at the table but, still glowing from his successful afternoon, he seemed inclined to regard his son with forbearance.

"You're late, Natty," he remarked. "But I expect it took you a while to write down the entry for today. Did you bring the book down?"

"I forgot." Natty himself heard the faintness of his voice. He was afraid to look at his father. After he had sat down, he asked, "Do you want me to get it now?"

"No. We'll have supper first." Mrs. Hollins had come in from the kitchen, bringing lamb's kidneys on toast, hominy cakes, and a dish of the string beans that Mrs. John had canned during the summer. It was a supper designed to please Mr. Dunston, especially broiled hominy; he admired the beans, because they came from the farm garden, and sent Mrs. John his compliments. In contrast to the silence he usually maintained during their meals together, he was quite talkative, making plans for the return to the city.

"You must be sure to have your trunk packed soon after breakfast, so Jody can take it and mine over to the depot. And I'll have him box our partridges so they can be expressed with the trunks. Can you tell which birds are yours?"

Natty nodded.

"Then I'll give you two baggage tags to mark them, so you can claim credit when we eat them," Mr. Dunston continued. "Mother will certainly be impressed."

Natty did not find the idea of impressing his mother with two dead birds appealing. His mind was desperately calculating the time that remained to him.

"Did you hear what I said?" demanded Mr. Dunston. "You've hardly eaten a thing. Or said anything, either. Don't you feel well?"

"Not very," Natty managed to reply. For an instant he entertained an absurd hope that his father might tell him to go to bed. But instead Mr. Dunston excused him from dessert. "I know you don't like custard," he said with an air almost of indulgence. "Bring your candle and then go up and get the game record. I'll get the fire going in the living room and we can look at the book then."

[*174*]

The worn routine of having his candle lighted for him had become a hideous mockery. It made spurious the note almost of fellowship in his father's voice. As he climbed the stairs, step after step, he knew himself to be doomed. His father would take a few minutes to finish his supper and light the fire. He would wait a minute or two more before coming to the foot of the stairs to shout a summons in his ringing voice. Natty could not bear to think of that happening while Mrs. Hollins was still in the house.

But Mrs. Hollins was on the point of leaving. She always cleared up the kitchen while Mr. Dunston and Natty ate, so when they were finished there were only the dessert plates to wash. And now Natty heard her footfalls on the kitchen porch below his bedroom. Looking from the window, he saw the buggy lantern dimly illuminating the rump of the Hollinses' horse and Mr. Hollins himself. Almost at once Mrs. Hollins's shadowy figure crossed the lawn and entered the lantern light as she climbed to the seat beside her husband. The horse started up, turning towards the pond and the road up to the flatland. Time had run out.

Natty picked up the book from his desk, pausing to look once more through the window. The Hollinses' lantern was no more than a spark far up the hill road and, as he watched, it flicked out.

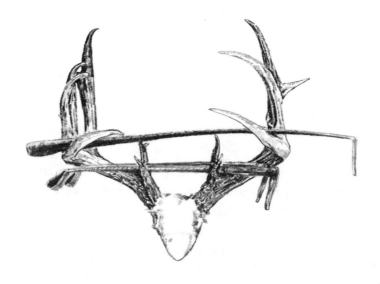

THIRTEEN

❧ THE WINDOW SHADES had been pulled down. Mr. Dunston was in his armchair at one side of the hearth, his eyes apparently lost in the blazing fire. But he looked up at Natty's entrance and said almost mildly, "You've been quite a while. Never mind. Let's look at the record."

Natty's hands were shaking, but his father appeared not to notice. "Sit down," he said, putting the book on his knee and taking his spectacles from their case. After placing them on his nose, he took them off again, to wipe them, before once more hooking them over his ears. Then he crossed his legs, his golf stockings with their patterned turn-over cuffs showing to the best advantage. It was the kind of production he liked to stage before he occasionally read to his children in place of their mother. He hadn't the faintest premonition of what he was about to find. He cleared his throat, as if he were going to read aloud, and opened the notebook, quite unaware of Natty's gaze, trans-fixed and frozen as a bird's before a snake.

His look of surprise changed to incredulity as he turned the second and third pages. Then his face suffused with anger and he turned his eyes on Natty.

"You've been lying to me these past weeks."

His voice was tight, pitched higher than Natty had ever heard it.

"You've lied to me every single day. Do you deny that?"

"No," Natty said, barely above a whisper. Now, when it was too late, he thought how simple it would have been to do what his father wanted and he wondered why he had not. His eyes glazed, he watched his father as if from far away. Mr. Dunston, his flush deepening, continued to turn the blank pages of the notebook. Then he stopped and Natty knew he had found the entry of his own day in the woods.

"So you killed both your birds with one shot, did you? But I distinctly heard two. You allowed me to think you had killed them with two shots. Didn't you?"

"Yes," Natty said.

"Well, which is it?"

"I killed them with one shot," Natty told him. "I didn't think you would believe that, so I fired off a second shot after."

"I find it easier to believe that you made one preposterously lucky shot than two successive good ones," Mr. Dunston said with biting sarcasm. "Still, the fact remains that you have lied and lied. I told you I would not tolerate a liar in my family. You have deliberately chosen to be one. So you will have to take the consequences. Go to the sofa and take your trousers and drawers down."

He was already on his feet and, before Natty could get himself out of his chair, taking down the African quirt.

"Dawdling won't do you any good," he said. "Don't make me wait."

Natty fumbled to undo his belt buckle and shove down his pants. He felt his drawers sticking again to his rump. He hesitated before trying to take them down.

"By God," his father exclaimed. "Bend over."

As Natty did so, Mr. Dunston grasped the waistband of his drawers and yanked them down. The pain made Natty cry out. He waited, all his bodily functions now on the trigger to let go as he tried for a moment anyway to keep them under control.

But there was no swish of the quirt coming down. An instant later Mr. Dunston said, "Stand up and look at me."

He turned to his father.

"Do you realize how truly evil your behavior has been?" Mr. Dunston said. "You have not only lied to me. You have chosen to deceive me in other ways. Besides, you have hurt me. Hurt me very badly. *Wounded* me. I never thought a child of mine would treat me so. It's more than any man should be asked to bear."

Natty heard the mounting anger in the voice and tried to prepare himself for what was coming, but his father said abruptly, "In spite of that, I have decided to give you a choice." He paused. Natty said nothing. "Are you interested?"

"Yes." To his astonishment, Natty found that he could meet his father's contemptuous blue stare. He saw something behind it he had never seen before.

"I will give you a choice, either of taking the whipping you deserve or giving up that dog of yours."

Natty found nothing immediately to say.

"Well," Mr. Dunston demanded peremptorily. "Which?"

"I'll give up Bingo."

His father dropped the quirt to the floor. "I guessed as much. To save your skin you are willing to let your dog go." His voice quivered with contempt. "A fine, upstanding, courageous boy! Good God!"

But now, Natty had recognized the uncertainty behind those staring blue eyes. His father had no way of knowing that he had already found a better place for Bingo than their own farm, where a nondescript small shepherd would never be accepted. And in spite of the bitter, scornful words, he was swept by a wave of pity for his father as well as himself, for he saw with appalling clarity how they both had diminished themselves.

FOURTEEN

✿ NATTY woke to a feeling of emptiness and, strangely, of peace. By some indefinable process of reasoning, he was sure that the relationship with his father had changed, that the confrontation of the past weeks would never be repeated. Mostly, however, he was surprised that he had been able to sleep so soundly and so late. It was already past breakfast time. From the front of the house he heard footfalls, then heavy, careful breathing, and realized that it had to be Jody and Lincoln John taking his father's large, khaki-colored trunk downstairs. In a minute or two they would be coming for his own. If he hurried he would just have time to get his clothes on.

"Your trunk ready, Natty?" Lincoln John asked.

"Yes," Natty said. "I finished packing before I went to bed."

Last night, his father had replaced the quirt on the deer horns and turned to his desk without speaking, and after a moment, Natty had left without saying good night. He had found his way upstairs and down the hall to his room in the dark, feeling along the wall with one hand, carrying his candlestick in the other. In his bedroom he had groped for his matches in the bureau drawer and lighted his candle. He had not closed his bedroom door, nor did he hide away the matches, but left them in the candlestick. Then he had finished packing his trunk.

Mr. John and Jody now picked it up together and went along the hall to the front stairs. By the time Natty reached the kitchen, the trunks were loaded onto the spring wagon and Jody was on his way with them to Boonville. It was insignificant compared to the sending-off when the whole family was leaving for the winter. Then the trunks belonging to his mother and his father, his brother, his sister, and himself, and the huge affair that Mrs. Dunston called the "household trunk," together with the fat, strapped valises and baskets of the maids, were loaded on the light lumber-wagon and

Lincoln John himself took them to the depot. With only two trunks to be checked, Jody was apparently considered competent. But to Natty it seemed just as much the ending of a season — in some ways even more final, for he would have to take Bingo to the Hollinses' farm.

Yet for as long as he could, he kept to their usual routine. The pup ate his breakfast on the kitchen porch, they took the letters down to the mailbox; later, when the thud of the river-bridge planks gave warning, they went down again to fetch the mail. It was just as it had been every day all summer. Mr. Lewis admired the way Bingo was "coming on," took the letters from Natty, and handed over the mail he had been carrying. But then Natty had to say good-bye.

"You're going back to New York City?"

"Yes," Natty said. "Tonight."

"Well," Mr. Lewis said, "I'll miss you, but I'll look forward to seeing you two here next summer."

"It'll be just me," Natty told him. "I'm going to give Bingo away. To the Hollinses. They need a cowdog, now Redskin's dead."

Mr. Lewis looked at him with eyes that were kind but unusually penetrating. Then, after a minute, he said, "I see. It won't be quite the same though, without the two of you waiting here."

"No."

Mr. Lewis smiled and the old horse pulled away without any other word spoken. But as he walked back up the drive with Bingo racing on ahead, Natty felt better. He asked Mrs. Hollins whether Herschel and Mr. Hollins would be around the place.

"They're digging potatoes up on the flats this morning," she answered. "But they'll be home for their lunch."

Since the Hollinses always ate at noon, while Mr. Dunston had his luncheon at one o'clock, Natty decided it would be best to take Bingo over then. They walked abreast along the road, Natty in one wheel track and Bingo in the other, with the dividing runner of grass between them. The young dog showed no inclination to make his usual forays into the woods, as if he had foreknowledge that some sort of change was in store for him; and he and Natty were still side by side as they came up to the buildings of the Hollinses' place and found Herschel and his father unloading their morning's harvest into the potato cellar beyond the end of the house.

They stopped work as Natty came up to them. "I've brought Bingo."

"I see you have," Mr. Hollins said. "We're glad to have him. As soon as we're done here, we'll take him over to the barn."

With the last potatoes in the cellar, Mr. Hollins covered the opening while Herschel drove the wagon to the barnyard. Bingo went with him, trotting along beside a rear wheel. Mr. Hollins and Natty followed.

"Looks like that pup will settle in all right," Mr. Hollins said.

"He likes Herschel," Natty said.

Herschel unhooked the team from the wagon and led them into the barn to put them in their stalls. Bingo went in also. When Mr. Hollins reached the stable entrance, he called, "Stay there awhile, Herschel, and keep the dog interested." The trollies rumbled on the track above the door as he pulled it shut. He looked down at Natty.

"It's best for you to go while Bingo feels he's busy with Herschel and the team," he said. "We're glad to have him here. And thank you kindly, Natty."

Mr. Hollins smiled, which was something he didn't often do. It brought Natty a good feeling. He said, "Bingo's lucky to get a home here, Mr. Hollins. My father doesn't think much of him. He said last night I had to give him to somebody else. He didn't want him on our place anymore."

"Well, he didn't know you'd said already you would give him to us, I guess," Mr. Hollins said. "Maybe it's best he doesn't know. We won't any of us tell him, ever. Your dog's here and now he belongs to us and that's all there is to it."

Looking up into his eyes, Natty suddenly felt close to crying. Mr. Hollins, still smiling, added, "It's hard sometimes when something has to end, Natty. But like as not, that's just about the time something new will be beginning for you."

He reached down and shook hands, and Natty turned away for home, taking Herschel's secret path down the little hill to the river road.